OUTLAW RUN

Ben had just reached the edge of town when two riders appeared out of the gloom on the prairie. Their horses were fatigued and trail dust was heavy on their clothes. Ben nodded politely as they passed.

"Howdy."

"Howdy," one replied. "Is the jail on the main street?"

Ben caught sight of the flicker of a badge under the man's vest. These would be the U.S. marshals sent to pick him up. "Nope," he lied. "You'll find it over on the far edge of town."

The lawman cursed under his breath.

"Thanks, mister," his pard said.

Ben continued on, and when the time was right he flicked the reins across the horse's shoulders and urged the animal into a gallop. The old thrill welled up in his emotions once more.

The run was on again.

PATRICK E. ANDREWS

DESPERADO RUN

ZEBRA BOOKS
KENSINGTON PUBLISHING CORP.

ZEBRA BOOKS

are published by

Kensington Publishing Corp.
475 Park Avenue South
New York, NY 10016

First printing: May 1987

Printed in the United States of America

This story begins on a ranch in the Texas Panhandle during a dark, moonless August night of the year 1901. . . .

Prologue

Through naked instinct Ben Cullen's eyes opened wide even before his brain could comprehend the reason for the action. It was a reflex of perceived danger that had never let him down in the thirty-six years of his life.

In a matter of seconds, his senses were a hundred percent alerted, and he glanced around the dark bunkhouse. At first all he could hear was the heavy breathing and snoring of the other ranch hands who slept in the crude beds located alongside the walls. But within moments Ben could sense movement — not *inside* but *outside* the rustic structure used to house the work crew.

He slipped quietly out of his bunk and eased himself to a spot beside the window. Taking care not to reveal himself, he looked out into the dark night. At first his eyes could only discern the regular features of the landscape in the deep shadows. The windmill down by the corral barely showed against the inky sky, but as his eyes grew used to the moonless scene before him, Ben caught a flicker of movement in the somber environment.

Then another—and another.

There was no doubt a sizable group of men were in the immediate area, and they were closing in on the bunkhouse. Ben, always ready and packed, moved back to his bunk and quickly but quietly dressed. After buckling on his pistol belt and grabbing his Winchester carbine and saddlebags, he went back to the window for several more moments of observation.

The subtle activity in the darkness had not only increased, but this time it was decidedly closer.

Ben eased the swinging window open and slipped through it, stepping silently to the ground. He quickly squatted in the dark shadows, becoming as motionless as a puma ready to pounce. Short and bandy-legged, his small stature came in handy during times like this when concealment made all the difference between freedom and a sheriff's cell.

After several long moments of listening, he felt confident he had spotted all the men moving in. He chose another spot and moved silently to it once again to sit and wait. By keeping his head close to the ground and peering upward he could spot even the barely visible silhouettes of the posse against the dark sky.

After a few short moments, Ben was fully aware of the two yokels nearby who thought they were well concealed.

"When we moving in?" a coarse whisper asked a nearby companion.

"Pretty quick I reckon," the other answered.

"I hear that Cullen's a mean little bastard."

"Yeah. Ever see him?"

"Nope. Can't say that I have."

"I did in New Mexico once," the lawman remarked. "Got a big ol' scar on his cheek. A Mezkin did it to him. They say Cullen took an ax to him for it."

"Oh, yeah! I heard about that."

Ben, listening to the low-toned exchange, shook his head in wonder at the crazy story. He quickly turned his mind back to his present predicament. There was only one logical place the manhunters could leave their horses without approaching close enough for the animals to give them away. That would be at a stand of cottonwoods that rose from the bare prairie some two hundred yards away.

Ben chose that as his destination.

Barely breathing, he glided without a sound across the ranchyard, under the fence, and out into open country. It only took him ten minutes to reach the place.

A gawky youngster, clumsily hanging onto a shotgun, had been posted as guard at the impromptu horse picket. The kid stared off into the darkness obviously anticipating the fireworks expected to break within a quarter of an hour as his fellow outlaw chasers positioned themselves.

Ben, barely breathing, snuck up behind the young sentry with his Winchester ready.

The barrel crashed into the kid's head. Ben quickly grabbed his victim to gently lower him to the ground in order to avoid the sound of a falling body. The youngster's head lolled loosely on his shoulders, but Ben didn't have time to put him into a comfortable position. He wasn't able to leisurely pick a good mount either. He could only hope he got a good one, full of spit and grit.

The hunted man untied one of the horses and walked it away toward the west. When he was certain he was out of earshot, he swung up into the saddle and kicked the horse's flanks.

The run had begun.

Chapter One

The horse whinnied impatiently and stomped a hoof despite Ben's gentle stroking of its muzzle. The two stood in an arroyo that marked the location of some long-ago creek that had once flowed down into the valley that stretched out below them.

Ben knew the posse tailed him by approximately a half hour, but he wasn't positive of their location or direction of travel. He decided it best to find a place of concealment until another day went by or the pursuers showed themselves, giving him a clear look at their intentions and directions.

He had just finished brushing away tracks and piling vegetation up in the arroyo's entrance to break up its distinct outline from view when he spotted the lawmen riding over the horizon at a steady pace.

From the way they were stretched out in a wide-gapped line, he knew they either hadn't actually picked up his trail or had lost it momentarily and were searching for signs indicating his direction of travel.

Ben's plan of escape was supposed to take him eventually into the Kiowa country of Oklahoma Territory. He had run guns and liquor in there before—

particularly the latter since the turn of the century — and knew he could find some shelter among Indian friends at best, or a lonely hideout in the wild country at worst. The fact that the posse had begun veering south, showing that they thought he must be heading that way, confused him. If he were chasing a man in that part of the country, Ben would naturally assume the quarry would seek the wild sanctuary of the Indian Territory.

Another thing had bothered him for some time as well. He couldn't identify the source of the sense of uneasiness that made him irritable and jumpy, but something was definitely wrong.

These gut feelings had dominated his decisions for the past twenty years. At age thirty-six, he had spent only ten years of his adult life as a relatively free man, but he credited those ten to instincts not only for survival but also for freedom. Those same mysterious sensibilities had awakened him the previous night as the posse closed in on him; now they were giving him further warning, but he couldn't discern the danger no matter how hard he tried.

Ben attempted to ease his nervousness a bit by checking out the saddlebags of the horse he had stolen. The leather containers revealed a couple of cans of beans, beef jerky, a tin box of crackers, and miscellaneous condiments. A full canteen of water was draped over the saddlehorn. For a light-eating, skinny man like Ben Cullen, even that scant fare would last him quite a while.

As Ben leisurely checked out the change of clothing stuffed into the other side of the bags, the reason for his uneasiness leaped into his consciousness.

When he'd snuck up on the kid and stolen the horse, he had noted there were twelve animals tied up there. But when the posse rode by on the valley floor he had counted but nine. True, he had stolen one of the dozen, leaving eleven; the injured guard's absence would cut the number to ten. That meant one of the manhunters was not accounted for.

Ben thought for several long moments, then relaxed as he figured that the missing horseman had probably been tasked with taking the hurt man back to the home folks. Ben grinned at his nervousness.

"Hold it, Ben! Don't you move a muscle!"

Ben, recognizing the voice, froze in mid-motion. "How are you doing, Jack?" he asked.

"Never mind, you scrawny little bastard," the other man said. "Now turn around real slow, hear?"

Ben complied and found himself facing an old adversary. U.S. Deputy Marshal Jack Macon, sweat streaking out of his battered Stetson, held the Winchester steady on Ben's middle.

"You sonofabitch! You're gonna hang now," Macon said.

"It's nice to see you again too, Jack," Ben said calmly. "And I ain't done no hanging offense."

"That boy you hit last night died."

Ben swallowed hard, but kept his expression calm. "Hell, he wasn't dead when I left him."

"That don't mean nothing," Macon said. He quickly added with a snarl, "Anyhow, maybe I oughta drill you and save the taxpayers the cost of some rope."

"I didn't mean to kill that kid," said Ben.

"Well, asshole, what you meant and what you did was two different things." Macon grinned at Ben's

13

discomfiture. "You're pekid, Ben. All the years is finally catching up to you."

"You don't look so good yourself, Jack," Ben said.

The lawman fished in his belt as he kept his eyes and weapon trained on Ben. After a few seconds he produced a set of handcuffs and tossed them over. "Snap 'em on," Macon said. "You know the routine by now. I'll push 'em tight."

"Front or back?" Ben asked in a calm voice.

"Front."

Ben moved back and deliberately stepped on a large rock protruding from the ground. He staggered to one side and sat down. "Shit! I twisted my ankle, Jack."

"Git up!"

"I can't, Jack. I hurt myself," Ben insisted.

"Get up, you sonofabitch, or I'm gonna shoot you *right now*!"

Ben quickly scrambled to his feet. "Don't shoot me, you hear, Jack? There ain't no reason to shoot me."

Macon moved closer. "On second thought, clap them cuffs *behind* you. And lemme tell you now, I ain't putting up with none o' your tricks. Put the cuff on your right wrist first, then put both hands behind. You'll ride that way all the way into Amarillo."

"Sure, Jack," Ben said. "Now there ain't no reason to shoot me, is there? I told you I didn't mean to kill him anyhow."

"You shouldn't have hit him so hard," Macon said.

"Looky here, Jack. I'm doing it like you say," Ben said. He locked the cuff over his right wrist and moved both hands behind him.

"Stand steady, you little— *Oh, Jesus Christ!*" Macon staggered back with the knife stuck deep in his upper abdomen.

Ben charged forward and swarmed over the larger man, forcing him to the ground. He wrenched the carbine free from the other's grasp and stood over the heavily bleeding marshal. "I always keep a knife back there," Ben said. "I thought you remembered that — and the fact I can sink it into anything within fifteen feet at the flick of an eye."

Macon groaned and rolled over. Ben knelt down beside him. "This is it, Jack. There ain't no way in hell you're getting outta this. You know that, huh?"

"Damn! You little turd! You cut me deep," Macon said.

Ben pulled the knife free and held the bloody blade up. "I done time and I won't do no more," he said. "And I sure ain't gonna take a hanging either."

Macon groaned. "Aw, shit, Ben! The kid ain't dead. I was just—" He stopped, his eyes widening. "Shit! It's burning in my gut."

Ben was angry. "What the hell you talking about, Jack? You stupid bastard. You told me I killed him!"

"I wanted to put a worry in you," Macon said. He gestured toward his horse. "I got bandages in my saddlebags."

Ben fetched the medical supplies and returned to the injured man. "It's your fault, you sonofabitch." He knelt down beside Macon and gave the wound a close inspection. "Jesus! You're really bleeding, Jack."

"Sweet Lord, Ben," Macon gasped. "I ain't gonna make it."

Ben agreed with him. "No, you ain't. You're leaking like a busted dam."

Macon's eyes opened wider in pain, but quickly

glassed over as his life's blood drained away to flow over the rocks as water had once done in that ancient creekbed.

"Wanted to put a worry in me, did you? Well, that worry got you killed, so it's all your fault," Ben said again. He hated Jack Macon, but he respected the lawman nevertheless. Ben figured he at least owed him a final gesture of honor, so he stood up and removed his hat. After a few moments he replaced it, then turned and hurried to his horse.

Although Ben Cullen's destination was the Indian Territory, he planned a stop at a special spot along the way. This was a permanent camp in a desolate area on the eastern side of the Texas panhandle.

The place was well known among outlawry simply as Paco's. It was a trading post of the most primitive sort. Nobody actually owned or ran the place, but a Mexican by the name of Paco Chavez was the focal point of attention there.

This criminal entrepreneur's specialty was stolen livestock. Whether it be a single animal or whole herds, Paco could find a buyer or a method of disposal—for a fee—and make the business of cattle or horse thieving profitable, safer, and easier. He lived under austere circumstances in a shack with his wife Florita, who was the offspring of a captive white girl and a Comanche warrior.

But rumor and small talk among the outlaws had it that Paco was actually the scion of a wealthy Mexican family and, during his absence from the camp, lived in regal splendor on a hacienda just across the Rio Grande in the Mexican state of Chihuahua. Supposedly he had another wife—the daughter of a wealthy Mexican politician—and children in this alter life. Paco's obvious refinement and education seemed to back up the assumption, but he would neither confirm nor deny it and tended to treat even the most casual of inquiries into his background as serious breaches of etiquette.

The place wasn't too crowded as Ben rode in on a warm evening. A few campfires being used by the usual groups of casual visitors cast thin, drifting clouds of smoke through the redbuds and willows along the creek that snaked its way through the sprawled, unorganized campground. Ben nodded to a few people he recognized, but saw no one he could call an old friend. Finally he stopped in front of Paco's cabin. Florita, who preferred to do her cooking outside, stirred at a pot of venison stew as Ben dismounted.

"Howdy, Florita," Ben said. "Is Paco to home?"

The woman pointed at the shack and continued her task. Ben never could see what the Mexican saw in the half-breed woman. She was surly, barely spoke, and was showing a growing tendency to plumpness although he had to admit her high Indian cheekbones combined with pale hazel eyes did give her a sort of sensuousness.

"Hey, Paco," Ben called and banged on the shack's door.

"Yeah?"

"Ben Cullen."

"Flacito!" Paco called using the Spanish nickname he had for Ben. It meant "skinny" and fit Ben well. The Mexican invited him inside with a shouted, *"Entra, amigo!"*

Ben went into the shack and found his old friend seated at a rickety table with a bottle of tequila and a tin cup in front of him. It had been almost three years since he had seen the Mexican, and it was apparent that the progression toward obesity wasn't confined to the wife alone in that family. Paco's face had lost its hard sharpness and was round and pudgy, but his enormous black moustache still turned magnificently upward in proud curls.

Ben offered his hand. "How are you, *amigo*?"

"*Muy bien*," Paco answered. "You want some tequila?"

"Sure," Ben answered.

"Then get a cup off the shelf there, eh?" Paco said. "You want to get drunk?"

"I reckon," Ben answered with a grin. "I ain't been able to lately."

"*Qué pasa*, you been broke?"

"Nope," Ben answered, pouring himself a half cup of the fiery liquor. "I been laying low like. Had a job on a ranch a ways west o' here fer a few months, but somebody musta blowed the whistle on me. So I'm on the run again."

"*Lástima*, too bad, Flacito," Paco said. "But you can stay here for a while, if you want. What do you say?"

"I thank you kindly," Ben said. He motioned to the tequila. "How come you're drinking? You got something to celebrate?"

"Celebrate, *mierda*!" Paco swore. "This old world of ours is going to hell."

"I know what my troubles is," Ben said. "What's your particular problem?"

"Civilization," Paco answered. "That's my problem. All the open country is getting cut up into farms with

18

towns between them. It's harder and harder to move livestock anymore. You keep stumbling into somebody or a new settlement that's sprung up overnight. It's putting me out of business, Flacito."

"Yeah, things is changing, all right," Ben mused after taking a swallow of tequila. "Getting hard to run for the same reason. That's why I'm heading for Kiowa country in the Injun Territory."

Paco nodded. "Good idea for you. You got friends over there and know where to hide. It'd take an army to dig you out."

"Yeah," Ben agreed. "I thought I'd drop off here on the way and see if there was anybody I knowed around. O' course I wanted to hear the latest about what's going on since I been outta touch."

"There ain't nothing going on — *nada* — until we can work out a way to carry on our business," Paco said. "But I don't think we can."

"Then, I don't reckon I'll be staying long," Ben said. "I'd best be back in the saddle mighty quick."

"It'd be better if you slept here tonight," Paco suggested. "Might as well get some rest while you got the chance."

"Thanks," Ben responded. "I'm gonna be riding long and hard before I get to where I'm headed."

Paco lit a cigar. "Then, let's have a few drinks, my old *compañero*, and we'll talk of former days — days of glory and danger — when men were men" — he laughed — "and the women were glad of it!"

"I'll sure as hell drink to that," Ben said, raising his tin cup.

Florita came in and wordlessly served both men generous amounts of the stew, then returned outside to eat by herself.

Ben watched the woman leave. "You reckon she'll ever be fully civilized?"

"No," Paco said shaking his head. "But when a man lives out here, she's the only kind of woman to have, *verdad*?"

They consumed the meal quickly and pushed the bowls aside to begin an evening of slow talk that was only interrupted when Paco went outside to order Florita to unsaddle Ben's horse and put the animal in their corral. Then he returned to the table.

The two men barely admitted they were in the twilight of their lives. Both had yet to reach the age of forty. But they knew that the encroachment of culture and its law and order was bringing their way of life to a close as sure as if they were doddering ancients in their nineties.

The evening ended with more reminiscences until they finally left the table to settle in for the night. Ben used his saddle and blankets—dutifully brought in by Florita—to bed down on the floor. He sank into a deep, dreamless sleep.

Toward dawn, Ben was instantly aroused by Paco's hand on his shoulder. "Shhh," the Mexican cautioned his friend. "You are going to have to leave *pronto*, Flacito."

Ben, who had slept fully clothed, got to his feet with his Winchester in hand. "What's going on?"

"There's some of the boys here that's got an interest in you," Paco explained. "Seems there's a reward, Flacito, and things are tough enough they mean to haul you in—dead or alive."

"Goddammit!" Ben cursed. In the back of his mind

he'd known that killing Marshal Jack Macon would bring him grief. He started to ask how Paco had found out there were men in the camp after him but he noticed Florita standing by the door. Obviously the woman kept on the alert and had either overheard a plot or been told of it by someone looking for a favor from her husband.

"I'd best see to my horse," Ben said.

"He's ready," Paco said. "I had Florita saddle him up for you."

"Obliged, Paco, I sure as hell appreciate this," Ben said. He walked toward the door and looked at the Mexican's wife. "Thanks, Florita."

The woman looked at him stonily without acknowledging the expression of gratitude.

With a final wave, Ben went outside and leaped into the saddle. He pulled his hat down low over his face and let the horse meander to the western edges of the camp. Then he slapped the reins and galloped like hell for the open country as daylight eased over the eastern horizon.

Ben rode hard across the rise above the camp and dipped down into the prairie country before he settled the horse into a steady gait.

He managed to ride half the morning before they caught up to him. It was a clever ambush, brought off by men used to fighting and hiding on the wide openness of the plains. With no vegetation, they had used the rolling elevations of the terrain to hide their presence until they could approach close enough for an all-out attack.

Ben unmercifully spurred his horse until the animal felt the panic of its rider and, in a bid to outstrip the wind, tore across the grass as its pounding hooves kicked clods of dirt high into the air.

But the slug from the Henry .44 brought Ben's mount down, and the rider suddenly found himself hurtling through midair before crashing painfully to the ground.

Chapter Two

Ben Cullen had been born and raised in the small town of Pleasanton, Kansas. Like most outlaws, he recalled his past life without a lot of happy memories. One of the most unhappy of these recollections had occurred some twenty-six years previously. At that particular time, Ben was ten years old. He had been watching through a picket fence at some children playing in their yard. His activity was interrupted by the high-pitched voice of an irritated woman standing on the porch of the house.

"Scat! Git!" she screeched.

Ben looked from the children to the woman with a quizzical expression on his face.

"I said *git*, boy!"

The severe-looking woman brandished a broom in his direction.

Ben, confused, looked around and behind him for a cat or dog. The words *git* and *scat* were for animals that one wanted to be rid of.

"You hear me, boy?"

"Ma'am?" Ben asked.

"I tole you to scat, didn't I?"

A portly, balding man in his shirt-sleeves came out of the house and stood beside the woman. "Who're you yelling at, Minerva?"

"Oh, it's that Cullen boy there. I don't want him around the kids. You'd think even a no-account mother like his could take better care of him."

"Trash! That's what that woman is," the man said. "Godamned trash!"

Ben had heard his mother referred to in derogatory terms before. He knew she lived a life completely different from most of the other women in town, but he knew of a few who were even more public about things his mother kept private. As usual, he swallowed his anger and ignored the gibes he really didn't understand.

By then the couple's children had turned their attention from playing to watch. The three of them trooped up to the fence. Ben smiled at them. He knew all three of the Beardsley kids—Oren, Maybelle, and Paul—from his casual and infrequent attendance at the local schoolhouse.

"Howdy," Ben said in a friendly tone.

"What're you doing here?" Oren Beardsley, the oldest boy and much larger than Ben, asked.

"Nothing," Ben answered.

"I told you to git, boy!" Mrs. Beardsley exclaimed again in her shrill voice.

Ben, whose young mind couldn't comprehend if she were serious about wanting him to leave or not, merely stepped back from the fence and stuck his hands in the pockets of his raggedy pants.

"Y'all want to play or something?" he asked the Beardsley kids.

"Not with you," Oren said. "You're a shit."

"I ain't," Ben said. He now fully sensed being unwelcomed, but a combination of stubbornness and pride made him ignore the truthfulness of the situation.

"Yeah! You're a shit," Oren said again. Then he laughed. "And you got a funny haircut too. Looks like somebody put a bowl on your head and cut around it."

"No it don't," Ben said.

Beardsley walked up to the fence. "Hey, boy, didn't you hear what you was told to do?"

"No, sir," Ben answered with a weak smile.

"You was told to git! Now, goddammit! *Git!*"

Ben, suddenly afraid, backed out into the street.

Oren gleefully yelled at him. "Go on, Ben Cullen, or I'm gonna chuck a rock at you."

"Chuck one at him anyway," the father said.

The boy immediately responded and Ben had to jump away from the missile. Others quickly followed as the other two children joined in the game and Ben was forced into an ignoble retreat.

He finally stopped running when he reached the edge of the small town. In that year of 1875 the settlement consisted of a growing number of residences as a small business district mushroomed to serve the farmers moving into the area. These tillers of the soil had taken advantage of the Homestead Act to establish themselves in new lives. They sowed their trust, sweat, and courage into the rich, fertile prairie earth with plows brought with them from worse lives back east.

Ben Cullen lived in a shack just outside of town with his mother and her most recent lover, a dark brooding Irishman named Flaherty.

Ben's own father, a veteran of the Union army, had established a farm in the area after the war. He had contacted a fever in the military camp life he'd followed for three years. No doctor could ever properly diagnose the exact sickness he suffered from, but it and the hard life of pioneer farming knocked him out. He succumbed to pneumonia brought on by a devotion to his livestock during a particularly brutal blizzard.

Mrs. Cullen tried running the farm with hired hands, but just didn't have the knack to make things come out to the better. She began selling the place off piece by piece until there was nothing left but a small parcel. Finally even that was gone and she took young Ben and moved into town. They lived reasonably well for a while, but when the money from the land sales finally gave out, his mother had to take in laundry and live on the handouts of more prosperous and charitable neighbors in order to survive.

By the time they were forced into the small shack they now called home, Mrs. Cullen had developed a fondness for drinking and had found that taking in lovers was more pleasurable than washing other folks' dirty clothes. She settled into an alcoholic haze filled with many males. These men trooped through in a seemingly endless parade of gamblers, saddle tramps, and other social misfits.

Ben, ignored most of the time, got along well with the majority of his mother's live-in companions, but now and then there would be one like Flaherty who made life more than a bit difficult for the little boy.

Sometimes on cold nights Flaherty would get tired of Ben's presence and banish him outside, where he would sit and shiver until his mother and the man would drink enough to either pass out or forget he wasn't supposed to be inside. Then, with numb hands and feet, he would snuff and wipe at his runny nose as he warmed himself beside the small fire in the shack's old stove.

Ben went to school when he could. But there seemed to always be errands or occasional odd jobs that took him away from gaining an effective education. But he liked the schoolhouse. It was warm and clean, and, even though he was always far behind the other children his own age, the activities were interesting and he was frequently praised by the teacher for even the limited progress he made during his sporadic attendance.

And it was at the school that he got his first crush.

Maybelle Beardsley, his own age, was a honey blonde with the brightest, bluest eyes he had ever seen. Always dressed in a starched, ironed dress with her golden ringlets dancing in the sunlight, she seemed all the sweetness and goodness a girl should be to a ten-year-old growing up fast on the frontier.

His casual passing of the Beardsley home that day he was run off had been carefully planned with the hope of being invited inside to play. While it was true Oren always picked on him at school, Ben figured the larger boy wouldn't do it at his own house. He fervently hoped to become friends with him so he could get closer to Maybelle.

But now, after the stinging humiliation of being run off like an unwanted stray dog, Ben went back to his mother's shack and squatted in the sun, his mind turning over the treatment he had just received.

Ben stayed there in a thoughtful reverie as the hurt swept over him like the north wind over an isolated ranch. He felt a cry coming on, but he forced it back down, gritting his teeth against the heavy feeling of sadness grabbing at his insides.

A quarter of an hour later he had his emotions back under the cold control he'd developed over his scant years. He stood up, glad the shack was empty, to go inside to see if there was anything left to eat.

Ben Cullen continued this unhappy life for several more years. But by the time he was sixteen years old, his lot had improved substantially. He had moved out of his mother's shack and away from the tormentors she took up as lovers. The boy had found a job at the local livery and feed store. The pay wasn't much, but he was given a room in the attic above the business. In spite of his small size, he handled the heavy work with a cheerful determination that earned him the sincere gratitude of his employer, Art Larkin.

Ben's work finally forced him to abandon forever his education, but his infatuation for Maybelle Beardsley never lost its intensity. Her father's dry-goods store was only two doors down from the livery and Ben was able to see her now and then. It seemed she grew prettier with each passing year, and Ben's life was devoted to his secret dream of someday winning her heart and love for his own.

He daydreamed of working hard and saving his money until he could open his own store. These fantasies never quite identified the line of business he was in, only the picture of himself in a fancy suit and shiny new shoes looking mighty prosperous to all the folks — particularly to Maybelle — as they walked by.

Then, in his mental theater, a financial disaster of sorts strikes the community. Like the business, this misfortune never quite identified itself in his mind, but the calamity forces the town into near bankruptcy. From the howling, weeping and hand-wringing townspeople, however, steps forth Benjamin Cullen, his face calm and sure with a steady set to his jaw and clear vision in his eyes.

As the local citizens gather about in a town meeting, with Maybelle seated very close, Ben stands up and begins, "Now listen, folks, here's what we have to do." The speech, also not clearly defined, is a humdinger that has all the answers to the dilemma. His talk ends with the people applauding, the businesses saved and Mr. Beardsley himself offering a blushing and smiling Maybelle's hand to him in gratitude and admiration.

Of course there were also the more action-oriented scenes in these reveries of Maybelle falling in love with him. His favorite, played over and over in his mind, began with a gang of bandits who attack and try to drag off Mr. Beardsley until Ben fearlessly wades into them and single-handedly saves the man. Maybelle, of course, then throws herself at him in love and worshipful thanks. Sometimes his imagination let Maybelle herself be captured, and he would ride out to deliver her from their slimy grasp and take her back into town amid the cheering accolades of an admiring citizenry.

But the heart is ever impatient and even a boy like Ben Cullen knew that his best bet to win the girl would be more conventional methods such as at dances or socials.

At the community's Annual Harvest Ball of 1881, Ben made the decision that the time had come for him to step forth and seriously begin courting Maybelle Beardsley.

And it would forever change his life.

He made a number of severe sacrifices over a period of months to save money. He skipped meals, sought no diversions, and hoarded every penny unless absolutely necessary to spend. At one time he had a bad cough, but he would not lay out a cent to purchase any patent medicine to relieve the illness. Finally, with the yearly dance — the biggest and most important in the community — only a couple of days away, Ben Cullen started spending the money.

He began with the purchase of a secondhand suit from the livery's owner. Mr. Larkin was even shorter than Ben, and he was half again as big around. While short in the sleeves and trousers, it tended to bag in the chest and especially the seat of the britches, but Mrs. Larkin took pity on him and kindly altered it so the suit fit decently. Ben had also spent some of his savings on a new shirt with a high stiff collar and an outdated, cheap cravat. But he went all out for his shoes. These had been at Beardsley's store and they were high-button two-tones with black bottoms and bright yellow tops. Ben thought they were the most elegant examples of footwear he had ever seen — no matter if they were a trifle large.

The final preparation was a trip to the barber shop on the afternoon of the grand social event. Ben didn't stint here either. He laid out a whole dollar and a quarter. Not only did he get a shave, but he had his hair carefully cut, oiled, and combed into a shiny arrangement that made him right up to style for Pleasanton, Kansas. In fact, all this made Ben quite a dandy; he was up-to-date and top-quality.

When the evening of the ball arrived, Ben carefully dressed in his room in the livery attic, taking care not to muss his hair. Again his mind conjured up visions of his successful courtship of Maybelle Beardsley. This time the scene was the dance hall — actually the local militia armory — and Maybelle casually glances around as Ben just happens to step into the door. Her eyes open wide in feminine admiration as he strides into the building resplendent in haircut, new suit, and shoes. The band suddenly begins playing and he turns to her and, in a manly voice, asks her to dance. Then, as they whirl about the floor, Maybelle Beardsley falls deeply and forever in love with him. After the dance he escorts her home where she nearly swoons with joy when he asks if he can become a regular caller at her house.

Reality was cruel at the very start of the evening. When Ben first entered the armory he couldn't see Maybelle anywhere. A quarter of an hour later, he caught a glimpse of her dancing with another fellow . . . then another . . . and another . . . until she finally took a seat among some other girls near the refreshment table.

Ben allowed himself a few moments to admiringly

drink in the sight of the girl he longed for. His heartbeat increased and the tender side of his emotions gave him a lump in the throat. Ben truly loved Maybelle, with a sweet longing and caring unusual for a boy so young. But the gentle feelings were there, and Ben wanted to let her know of them that very night.

Ben took a deep breath. Then he pushed his way through the party-goers and finally approached her. "How do, May—er, I mean Miss Beardsley."

Maybelle looked up and saw him. She displayed no pleasure at the sight, but she forced a polite smile.

Ben cleared his throat and made a slight bow. "Would you—uh—like to dance?" He gestured clumsily. "I mean, when there's—er—some music?"

Maybelle laughed. "That's the best time."

Yeah. I reckon. So—would you?"

"No, thank you. Maybe another time."

A feeling of the old hurt kindled itself within him, but Ben tried to ignore it. He smiled weakly. "Sure, later, huh?"

"Perhaps," Maybelle said.

Ben backed away with an uncertain expression on his face. He turned and joined some other loose fellows at the other end of the armory.

He asked her twice more and each time was refused. He decided it best to let a little more time slide by before he tried again. He made several trips to the punch bowl feeling very unsure of himself. He could not admit to himself what he knew was true: Maybelle Beardsley did not like him. His sacrifices and day-dreams of the evening were all for nothing. His thoughts were interrupted by another boy his age.

"Hey, you, Ben Cullen," he said. "Somebody wants to see you outside."

"Who?" Ben said.

"All I'm supposed to tell you is that somebody wants to see you in the alley," the boy said. Then he moved off.

Ben's spirits soared. Perhaps Maybelle wanted to meet him alone. Maybe she wanted to pour out her heart to him and let him know their feelings were mutual and a great love existed between them.

Ben hurried outside and walked around the building to the alley. He didn't find Maybelle but he did walk straight into Oren and a couple of his friends.

"Howdy, Oren," Ben said with a chilling feeling of foreboding.

"Hey, Ben Cullen, I got something to tell you," Oren said, pushing him back against the wall. "You know what it is?"

"No. I don't reckon I do."

"Well, I'm telling you to leave my sister alone," Oren said. "She wanted me to tell you not to ask her for no more dances. What do you think of that?"

Ben knew Oren was speaking the truth. He'd made a fool out of himself. Again, that stubborn pride got him into trouble. "I'll do as I please." It was a statement of hurtful defiance.

"Oh, you will, huh?"

Ben looked at the other boys now joining his tormentor.

Oren reached out and mussed his hair. "Hey!" he yelled looking at his hand. "You got your scalp smeared with lard?" He sniffed at it. "Whew! Smells

33

like a big, ol' thick bucket o' perfumed hog fat's been melted over you, Ben Cullen. Is that what it is? A bunch o' pig fat on you, huh?"

Ben didn't answer the ridiculous question. His hair was the same as every man jack's at the dance. And that included Oren Beardsley's.

"Hey, Ben Cullen, when I talk to you, you answer, hear?"

Ben remained silent.

"Hit him, Oren," one of the other boys said. "Teach him a lesson."

Oren complied and Ben's head snapped back. A second and third blow dumped him to the ground. Oren reached down and grabbed Ben's hair. "I'm gonna do you a big favor, Ben Cullen. I'll get that awful oil outta your hair." He picked up a handful of dirt and began rubbing it onto Ben's head. The effort created a muddy mixture in the heavy hair oil. Then Oren began pulling and tugging with wild giggling.

Ben, the pain unbearable and blinding, fought back as best he could. Oren continued the torment for several more moments before he finally ceased his efforts and stepped back.

Ben lay there, his scalp feeling as if thousands of hot needles had been pushed into it. He tried to get up but Oren pushed him back into the dirt.

"Now you stay away from Maybelle, you hear?" Oren said. "You're just trash, Ben Cullen. She don't want you embarrassing her no more by hanging around."

Then Ben was left alone as the others walked back to rejoin the dance.

He limped down the alley. The suit was a rumpled, dusty mess and his hair was full of dirt, some of which was on his face in muddy streaks. The feeling of anguish and humiliation was so great it seemed to squeeze the air from his lungs. As he walked along he noticed he was behind the Beardsley dry-goods store. Standing there, another emotion suppressed the hurt and embarrassment.

Ben Cullen became angry. Then that anger grew until he was uncontrollably infuriated.

He looked up and down the alley, then walked up to the back door of the business.

The memory of that moment was never clear to Ben. It was a lengthy spasm of an exploding, insane temper that ended with him being dragged down the street, kicking and bellowing, by the town sheriff.

His trial took place within ten days of his breaking into the Beardsley store. At the time his right eye was still swollen shut and the knot on his head had barely subsided. These injuries weren't from his encounter with Oren Beardsley. They were from tangling with the local law officer.

The charges against him were burglary, breaking and entering, destruction of private property, resisting arrest, and assault upon a law officer.

The courtroom was set up in the local saloon since the town hall was still under construction at the time. The judge, seated at a desk brought in for the occasion, directed activities from one end of the room. The jury was situated behind the bar proper while the witness chair had been placed next to the judge. The crowd assembled around the tables in groups as they eagerly anticipated the event.

Ben's lawyer was a local by the name of Harry Seed who displayed as much fondness for the bottle as he did for the practice of law. But, despite the seriousness of the charges, the attorney was unworried, and assured Ben that at worst he could expect ninety days' confinement and to be ordered to pay for the damages he did. Then the attorney settled back to nip at his flask as the proceedings went on.

The prosecutor, who traveled with the circuit judge and picked up his cases from the local sheriffs when he arrived in their towns, was a gaunt, dark, and somber man with the meanest eyes Ben Cullen had ever seen. He glared in righteous anger at the boy to such an extent that Ben instinctively slunk down in his chair.

Harry Seed smiled and tippled.

Sheriff Milburn Rawlins was the first witness. In response to the prosecutor's questions he testified: "I was on my routine rounds on the night of August 27, 1881, when I heard a noise in the Beardsley dry-goods store."

"Which is located in this town?" the prosecutor asked.

"Yes, indeed, sir," Sheriff Rawlins answered. "Anyhow, I looked through the winder and I seen Ben Cullen in there tearing hell outta the place."

"Is the aforementioned Ben Cullen in this room at this time?"

"He sure as hell is," Rawlins said pointing to Ben. "There's the no-good little sonofabitch!"

Henry Seed tossed off another drink from his flask.

Rawlins continued. "So I went in there and the kid

was going crazy. He was throwing stuff around and breaking up anything he could get his hands on. I told him to stop and the little bastard jumped on me. Well, I cold-cocked him with the barrel of my Smith and Wesson and drug him off to the calaboose."

The prosecutor, satisfied, turned to Seed. "Your witness."

Seed stood unsteadily. "Goddammit, Milburn, are you positive the kid you arrested was Ben Cullen?"

"Damn right!" Rawlins exclaimed.

Seed smiled at the judge. "Well, I'm sure as hell not gonna ask *him* no more questions." The crowd laughed and Seed waved to them as he sat back down.

The next, and final, witness for the prosecution was Oren Beardsley, who testified that Ben Cullen had been bothering his sister at the dance and that after a well-deserved thrashing, the cad had crawled off down the alley muttering curses and threats of revenge.

Henry Seed also had no questions for Oren and sat back to toss off a few more drinks until he was asked if the defense was ready.

"We are, Your Honor," he said standing up.

"Then begin."

"Yes, sir," Henry said, staggering a bit as he approached the bench to present his case.

"Hell, Your Honor, Ben Cullen is guilty as charged," Seed said. "There ain't no sense in denying that. But he's never been in trouble before and he was mad at Oren for beating him up like that. What he done was wrong and he's sorry as hell about it and throws hisself on the mercy of this here court. I'm positive you'll come up with the right ending to this whole affair." He walked back to Ben and turned to face the judge. "That's it."

The judge looked over at the prosecutor. "You want to sum up your case?"

"Think it's necessary?" he answered.

"Hardly," the judge said. He pointed to Seed and Ben. "Approach the bench."

Ben, his mind calculating how he would have to pay the Beardsleys out of his salary at the livery, had to hold Seed up as they stood before the judge.

"First off, I find you guilty of all charges," the judge said. "The worstest thing you done was to destroy private property, boy. This here country is based on the premise a man's home — and that means his private property — is his castle. What kind o' place would this be if ever' hard-working businessman got his place busted up whenever someone got riled at him? Well, I'll tell you — it'd be a mighty sad state of affairs. Then you was disrespectful to authority. That's law and order, boy, the thing that keeps us from being animals and preying on each other and living miserable, worthless existences in a world of ruin and chaos."

Ben, his head bowed, cringed before the bawling out as his lawyer stared down at the floor in a drunken reverie.

"You hear what I'm saying to you, boy?"

"Yes, sir," Ben answered in a somber voice. "And I truly regret —"

"Regret? *Regret*?" the judge exclaimed. "Boy, you're just about to learn what regret really is. I hereby sentence you to be confined in the Kansas State Penitentiary for a period of ten years at hard labor.

38

And while you're up there digging coal I want you to spend ever' day thinking on the wrongs you done."

"Ten years?" Ben asked in a quaking voice.

"Court adjourned!" the judge announced banging his gavel. Then he stood up and looked down at the small youth's pale face. *"Ten years!"*

Chapter Three

When the ambush had been sprung on him after leaving Paco's camp, Ben went down with the wounded horse. Now he sat up in the grass dazed, his head spinning and aching from being slammed into the ground. He felt extreme vertigo and confusion, but recovered in time to crawl low to the animal and drag the Winchester from its boot on the saddle.

As he scanned the horizon for signs of his attackers, he gave his mount a quick inspection. The stallion was clearly dying. A lucky shot had hit its neck just behind the jaw and evidently struck up into the horse's brain.

As his mind recovered from the fall, Ben became more alert. He realized he couldn't remain where he was. Recalling a small gully filled with deep, thick buffalo grass a short distance back, he eased down on his belly and inched toward its protection.

Ben stopped his progress every few moments to listen for movement around him. But there was only silence. Such soundlessness, when no prairie creature stirs nor a meadowlark sings, was a dead giveaway that there were intruders in this natural domain.

Ben wished he knew how many dry-gulchers there were out there. Like most small skinny men, he had a natural knack for silent movement. An old friend once had said that Ben Cullen could do the fandango on a tin roof wearing Mexican spurs and not make a sound. He crawled across the ground and finally eased himself down into the deep vegetation of the gully before he treated himself to a short breathing spell.

Then he went after the bushwhackers.

The depression he was in sank no more than three and a half feet into the prairie earth, but the buffalo grass growing in it was more than six feet high.

"He ain't here with the horse."

Ben froze at the sound of the voice. He turned back to face the direction he had just come from.

"Charlie! Dan! Did you hear me?" the voice yelled. "I said he ain't at the horse."

There was a lack of wit and intelligence in the voice and Ben knew a real slow thinker had come along for the ride.

"Can you hear me, fellers?" the voice yelled again. "Hey! Charlie! Dan! Where you at?"

Ben grinned. He figured Charlie and Dan were old-timers and right now were cringing in anger as their stupid friend not only gave himself away, but inadvertently informed their prey that there were three of them.

The sound of the dimwit thrashing through the grass faded away, then grew louder as he walked back and forth. "The feller's gone! C'mon out!" he hollered. "What're y'all waiting for, huh?"

Ben suddenly froze as he sensed movement behind him. He slipped through the grass to the opposite side of the gully and spotted a cantankerous old man, his features wearing a furious expression as he unknowingly crawled toward Ben. Ben took careful aim with the Winchester and fired. The oldster's frown disappeared as the heavy slug caved in his face and, at almost the same instant, took out the back of his head in a spray of blood and brains.

"Hey! Hey!" the dimwit yelled at the sound of the shot. "Who did that? Charlie? Dan?"

Ben squatted down and crawled without sound for twenty yards until he reached the opening end of the earthen slash he had been using for cover.

"Charlie! Dan! Where are you?" the dimwit pleaded. "Hey, this ain't a bit funny, huh? I'm getting mad, that's what I'm doing."

Ben remained quiet as the dimwit ran back and forth looking for his companions. He figured he would let the stupid bastard do his work for him. Eventually the dumb gunhawk would have to stumble across his surviving companion.

And, within five minutes, he did.

"Damn, Charlie! What are you doing down there?" the dimwit asked. "Didn't you hear me a-hollering for

42

you?"

"Shut up, you shitass!" the elusive Charlie cursed. "If you wasn't my cousin, I swear I'd shoot you."

"What's the matter?"

"I said *shut up!*"

"Where's that old fart Dan, huh? Did he fire that shot or did you?" the dimwit asked.

Ben's carbine kicked back against his shoulder and the bullet slammed into the man called Charlie, kicking him over on his back. A quick working of the cocking lever, another shot, and the final slug made the man's skull explode. Then Ben swung the muzzle toward the dumb one as he chambered another round.

"Hey!" the dimwit yelled stupidly. He looked down at his dead cousin then back at Ben several times trying to comprehend the reality of the dangerous situation he was in.

Ben walked up to him holding his carbine ready. "Drop your gunbelt!"

"Y-yes, sir," the dimwit said, hastily obeying.

"Y'know, I think you're prob'ly just about the dumbest sonofabitch I've ever run into," Ben said. "Why don't you take a walk back to where you came from?"

"I'd rather ride my horse."

"Well, you ain't getting your damn horse back," Ben snapped. "I could shoot you as dead as your pards, but I'm taking pity on you, you poor dumb shit-for-brains. Now, don't make me change my mind. Get moving — *now!*"

The dimwit hesitated, then began walking away. He looked back several times, but continued traveling until he disappeared over the horizon.

The entire episode turned out to be a blessing for Ben Cullen. Despite the bruises and the delay, he managed to get a better horse—after turning the other two loose—and the contents of the would-be ambushers' three saddlebags added to his larder and ammunition supply.

Without even a last look at the two dead men sprawled around in the general vicinity of the dying horse, Ben once against took up his western trek into the Indian Territory.

Ben rode all the rest of that day and into the night before he finally stopped and settled down into a simple camp to pass the night. The next morning, early and after a skimpy breakfast of coffee and beef jerky, he was once again bound for the safety offered in the land of the Kiowas.

Although there were no signposts, Ben knew when he had ridden into the area he had chosen for a hideout. The open wilderness and isolation from other people promised him almost-unlimited safety. He pushed on impatiently in the comforting desire of penetrating deeper into the wild country. He topped a rise and, in angry surprise, reined in so hard his horse whinnied a sharp protest.

Spread out before him in orderly rows of tents, shacks, and new buildings under construction was a brand new settlement—deep in the heart of the Kiowa country.

After staring at the scene for several moments, Ben decided the best thing he could do would be to ride in and assess the situation and find out what had been happening in the territory during his absence.

A tent, bearing a sign announcing it as the business establishment of an attorney-at-law, stood at the edge of the place. Charlie stopped his horse and looked down at the man standing in the opening of the canvas establishment. "What is this place? It must have just popped up here."

"It sure did, mister," the man pleasantly. "Let me be the first to welcome you to the town of Hobart, soon to be the pride of Oklahoma Territory."

The town of Hobart seemed as good a place as any to hide for a while. All of the people were new to the area and Ben Cullen found he could blend anonymously into the newcomers who labored to establish their new habitat.

Ben, with the money gleaned from his latest encounter, ate at the local cafes—mostly tents with plank counters sat up in front of them—and moved among the people as he firmed up plans. He avoided making friends or even becoming too well known, but he did adapt himself enough to the settlement to begin pronouncing the name of their town like the citizens. Although spelled Ho*bart*, it was pronounced Ho*burt* with the accent on the first syllable.

It hadn't taken Ben long to find out that Hobart was but one of the new towns in this formerly wild, untamed area. There were others: Mountain View, Lone Wolf, Harrison, and Parkersburg. The fugitive could only figure that other areas of territory that once belonged to the Indians were going through the same change. That left him with very few places to hide out.

Melting into the close-packed town also gave Ben another idea for escaping the law. All his life had been spent in the vast wilderness. With this sanctuary gradually disappearing, he figured it was time to change his tactics. If a provincial area like the country of Kiowa offered shelter, think of the great populated areas of the east, where entire cities beckoned to him. Ben Cullen could imagine the ease of pulling a robbery in a bank, then quickly melting into the teeming crowds or down narrow alleys as posses of city policemen vainly tried to mount a pursuit.

There were two matters to be taken care of before his move, however. First he had to pick a place to go, and that was easy. Old time cowboys had told him of trips to Chicago on cattle trains when they would accompany their herds to the great stockyards. There were crowded streets, tall buildings, and whole neighborhoods where the inhabitants didn't even speak English. Ben could imagine blue-clad policmen trying to ask some thick-headed foreigner, "Which way did he go?" as the confused immigrant merely scratched his head in ignorance.

The second matter he had to attend to was getting a grubstake to finance the move and allow him some time to get established and learn his way around before he began pulling off the numerous jobs he planned. A couple of hours of scouting around Hobart brought the solution to that problem. The answer was in the form of a two-storied frame building with a freshly painted sign proudly mounted on the false front that proclaimed it as the KIOWA COUNTY BANK.

Once the place was picked, Ben settled into a routine to carefully check it out. Through simple observation, a casual question here and there and listening to conversations, he learned a surprising number of things. The president of the new institution was W. T. Abernathy, a portly individual whose residence was located west of the business district in an easily identifiable small but well-built house with a picket fence around the yard; the bank's money was kept in one large safe in the building; the only guard was a bachelor carpenter named Ned Brownley who earned extra money by sleeping on a cot by the safe; and, finally, Abernathy was bragging how his bank now had assets totaling more than twenty thousand dollars.

By this time Ben's finances had sunk low enough that he had to make a move whether he wanted to or not. He took his last remaining dollars and bought some canned goods and other nonperishable items. During the purchases, he made numerous statements about leaving Hobart and striking south for Texas where he was going back to the family farm and pick up his "wife and young'uns" then return to Kiowa County to homestead. These remarks involved him in several inane conversations with locals, but he figured it worth the trouble if he would be dismissed from their minds as a possible suspect after the bank robbery. And if they did remember him with suspicion, their recollections would send any posses south into Texas looking for him, while he went north to Wichita, Kansas, where he planned on taking a train to Chicago.

Then, with all his money spent but his saddlebags loaded with food, Ben rode south of Hobart for several miles, then swung back east until he found a secluded spot where he could camp without being observed for two or three days.

With his horse hobbled but contentedly grazing on the thick, rich prairie grass, Ben settled down to wait. Part of his purchases had been a fifth of whiskey, and he sipped off the bottle and let his imagination—as active as it had been when he was a boy—take him to his new life in Chicago.

Ben pictured a street literally crammed with people along the sidewalks while wagons and buggies of every sort choke the avenue. A huge bank, located in a granite building on a corner, stands imposing and solid. Ben walks into the place and crosses the thick carpeting to a teller. The man, silent and thoroughly frightened at the sight of Ben's pistol, hurriedly fills several canvas bags with thick wads of bills. Then, in Ben's mind, he fires a number of shots into the ceiling and runs out the door. Pushing and shoving, he submerges himself into the shoulder-to-shoulder, teeming mass of people on the street until he extracts

48

himself to rush up to his hotel room and deposit the loot on the bed. There is at least fifty thousand dollars.

Beautiful!

On the third night following his departure from Hobart, Ben resaddled his horse, checked his guns, then rode through the darkness toward the east side of town where bank president W. T. Abernathy lived.

Chapter Four

After Ben's trial for breaking into Beardsley's store, the sixteen-year-old spent only a short time in the local lockup. A pair of marshals, who trailed after the circuit judge to pick up the sentenced prisoners left in his judicial wake, took Ben from the custody of the sheriff while curious townspeople gathered to watch.

Ben almost felt like a hero of sorts from the way people looked at him. His age peers displayed awe and respect as he was led from the town jail wearing handcuffs and leg irons. Although he shuffled awkwardly in the restraints, Ben displayed a bit of defiant bravado. Pride and a desire to show no fear motivated that appearance rather than pure courage.

The show ended, however, when the youngster was put into a large wagon with other prisoners. The vehicle had only small barred windows, and the summer heat made it stifling inside.

The trip to prison was one of pure agony with only occasional stops for water and the one meager ration issued daily by the uncaring escorts. The journey took eight days and they reached their destination one blistering hot afternoon.

Young Ben Cullen's first impression of the Kansas State Penitentiary was the sound of large metal portals clanging as they were opened. He sat in the suffocating heat of the enclosed wagon with a half-dozen other new convicts waiting to go into the prison yard when the loud noise startled him. Then the vehicle lurched forward and rolled about fifty yards before the team of horses pulling it were brought to a halt.

Next he could hear a large key being worked in a padlock, then the clanking of chains before the back door opened and a burly guard wearing a blue uniform bellowed in at them.

"All right, get out, get out, goddammit! I ain't standing here all day waiting for you sumbitches!"

Ben followed the example of the older men and scrambled out as quickly as he could. He was roughly pushed into a line with the others as he moved awkwardly in the handcuffs and shackles he had continued to wear since the beginning of his trip from Pleasanton.

One of the marshals who had accompanied them on the trip removed the restraints and tossed them back into the wagon. He turned to the prison guard. "They're all yours, Charlie. See you next trip."

"Yeah," the other responded. He pointed his cudgel at the prisoners, then swept it toward a foreboding gray building in front of them. "Get moving!"

Shorn of the bonds, Ben felt lighter and freer as he walked with the others in the indicated direction. The interior of the place was as unremarkable as the exterior, and they walked down a long hallway and turned into a room off to one side.

Two more guards had joined their original mentor, and the three, each holding a heavy club, seemed cold and aloof.

"Strip!" the senior of them commanded.

Once again Ben numbly imitated his companions and within moments stood naked in the heat of the windowless room.

A man wearing a suit suddenly appeared and, without ceremony, gave each a perfunctory physical examination which consisted of checking their teeth and making each demonstrate an ability to move their limbs freely and fully. Then, after a quick glance to see if any displayed any obvious signs of physical disability or illness, he turned to the chief guard. "All fit for hard labor." Then he left the room as quickly as he had come.

Another man instantly replaced him. This newcomer, a convict, went to each one with a pair of handclippers and unceremoniously clipped their hair down to the scalp leaving them bald with red spots where the crude, dull instruments had pulled at the sensitive skin of their heads.

"Let's go," the guard said.

Ben felt ill at ease walking out of the room naked, especially when one of the guards looked at him with a foreboding shake of his head.

Their next stop was a bathhouse where a convict duo, using a hand-pumped fire-fighting apparatus, hosed them down with icy water. For the first time since his confinement, Ben felt truly humiliated. The stinging spray on his bare skin seemed to emphasize the terrible, shameful predicament he was in.

Another naked walk down the corridor led them to a room where a long wooden counter stood. Behind this were piles of clothing and blankets. Another prisoner tossed various articles of wear at them along with a sack of toilet articles and two blankets.

"Put 'em on!" came the order.

Ben, grateful to be covering himself despite being wet, began to hurriedly dress. The clothing, which was too large for the boy, was remarkable in its unattractive black and white stripes. There was also a pillbox-type cap of the same design. When he'd donned the uniform, Ben felt ridiculous.

The guard who had given him the strange look walked up to him. "You been in prison before?"

"No," Ben answered.

"It's 'no, *sir*' and 'yes, *sir*' when you speak to a guard."

"No, sir," Ben said, correcting himself.

"Jesus!" the guard smirked. "By this time tomorrow, kid, you'll be a girl."

Ben, puzzled, continued to dress until he stood there in his striped apparel and, like the others, held his blankets and other belongings in front of him.

Another short walk took them to a room that held a wooden bench. The new convicts sat down and, remaining silent, waited to see what was next on the entrance agenda. For half an hour they sweated in the growing heat of the room before they were startled with a bellowed order to get to their feet. As they stood in anticipation, another man in a suit came into the room.

"This is Warden Hopkins," the head guard said as a way of introduction. "He has a few words to say. You listen up good."

Hopkins, a portly man with large whiskers, nodded curtly. "You're here because you've broken the laws of this state," he bluntly began. "For that you're being punished. If you want to avoid any further punishment, make sure you don't break the rules of this institution. For doing so, there are quick, unpleasant consequences. Those who try to get along will find their stay here relatively uneventful. Obey the regulations, the guards, and—most of all—me. By doing so you might even get a reduction in your sentence for good behavior."

Ben felt a glimmer of hope. Perhaps if he showed them he would be more than happy to obey any and all rules, his stay not only would not be too bad, but much shorter than the ten years the judge had ordered him to serve.

"Another way to improve your lot is to work hard," the warden continued. "The Kansas State Penitentiary is self-supporting through our coal mine. And we pay the convicts who labor there. For actually digging the coal, the state of Kansas will generously pay you a salary of one dollar and seventy-one and one-half cents a day. If you're assigned the task of pushing one of the carts, then you'll earn one dollar and twenty-three and two-thirds cents per day.

Ben was itching to get down in that coal mine and show what a marvelous worker he would be.

The warden handed the head guard a sheet of paper. "Here's the names and numbers." He turned back to the new convicts. "Remember what I said. Keep your noses clean and we'll treat you right. Make our lives unhappy and we'll make yours miserable. That's all."

The warden abruptly left. The guard called out their names and numbers with a warning to quickly commit them to memory. Later on the digits would be painted on their clothing.

Benjamin Cullen became Convict 2139.

When they left the room they went through a confusing system of barred doors that had to be locked and unlocked. Then they reached a building sporting two-storied tiers of cells. One by one each convict was checked into a cell and dropped off.

Ben, the last, found himself at the end of a row where he was ushered into an unoccupied cell. The other guards left, but the one who had spoken to him stayed. "The bunk is chained up to the wall. Undo it and it folds down," he explained.

"Thank you — sir," Ben said. He did as he was told and found that the wire contraption held a mattress stuffed with straw.

"The cap'n put you in this cell because he felt sorry for you," the guard said. "It'll take 'em longer to find you down here."

After another quick glance of genuine sympathy, he strolled away to his other duties.

Ben vaguely wondered what the man meant, but dismissed it from his mind as, sad and lonely, he sat his belongings up on a plank shelf anchored to the wall. He sat down on the bunk. At that moment he missed his room in Mr. Larkin's attic with such emotion he felt as if there were a large, empty hole in his heart. Since his troubles had begun, his mind had dwelt on Maybelle Beardsley for hardly a moment. The awfulness of her unkind rejection in the form of having her brother beat him up was something he couldn't bear to think about. Each time the girl's image entered his mind, he suppressed it as quickly as he could.

Now, utterly miserable and homesick, young Ben Cullen dully watched the shadows in his cell lengthen as the sun slowly descended through the summer sky.

Suddenly the sound of shuffling feet and clanging bars interrupted his dismal period of self-pity and he could hear many men — none saying as much as one word — walking in step along the tiers of the cell block.

A burly guard suddenly appeared at the bars. "2139?" the man asked gruffly.

"Sir?" Ben responded weakly.

"Goddammit! Didn't they tell you to learn your number?"

"Y-yes, sir, they told me," Ben stammered fearfully.

"Well, it don't look to me like you done the job very good," the guard said with a ferocious frown.

"My number's 2139," Ben quickly responded.

"Yeah. That's more like it," the guard said. "We go to chow in fifteen minutes. When the whistle blows, you step outside this cell, and from that point on you do as the others and keep your yap shut, understand?"

"Yes, sir."

The guard sensed he would have no troublemaker here, so he relaxed his mood a bit. "And, kid, don't talk in the chow hall either. Eat up quick and follow the leader."

"Yes, sir."

"You done any jailing before?"

Ben wasn't exactly sure what the man meant. "Well, sir, I ain't never been in any kinda trouble at all."

The guard's expression was one of genuine sympathy. "My God," he said under his breath. "What'd you do to get sent here?"

"I busted into a store," Ben said trying to be helpful.

"How many times?"

"Just once, sir. Like I told you, I ain't never been in

no trouble before."

The guard sighed. "Well, kid, you got troubles now."

Ben, a feeling of dread growing now, watched the man walk away. When the whistles blew, he did as he was told and stepped outside the barred door. He found himself in line with other convicts in their striped suits and, as a series of whistles gave the commands, the prison population moved silently, and in step, out of the building down to a communal dining hall.

The eating facility was a large area with long, narrow tables with the chairs all on one side so that everyone faced in a single direction. The meal, served in tin plates and cups with only spoons, consisted of beans, salt pork, and coffee. Although no one spoke, Ben noticed strange looks given him by a number of the men. Several smiled, a couple winked at him, and one made a gesture that could only be interpreted as blowing a kiss at him.

Ben quickly lowered his eyes in confusion, and ate his spartan meal.

The return to the cells was a reverse procedure and once again Ben was locked in. He lay back in the hot confines of his bare quarters and, using one blanket as a pillow, fell asleep.

It was still dark the next morning when once again the whistles blew and the prison awoke. After a trip to the dining hall—and more beans and salt pork—Ben Cullen, Convict 2139, was marched with others in a work detail across the prison yard and through several gates. The group was halted in the small, cluttered enclosure that bordered the mine entrance. Here Ben was assigned the job of pushing the empty coal cars down along the narrow-gauge track into the mine and bringing them back when they were filled up. Evidently he was going to be a $1.23^2/3$ man since he would do no actual digging of the coal.

The morning passed slowly as the small youth dug in his heels and strained with the loaded cars he pushed out of the mines. In spite of well-oiled wheels and the track, it was still hard work that made the hundred-pound feed sacks at the livery barn in Pleasanton seem like bags of fluffy feathers.

The midday meal was brought out to them — another feast of beans and salt pork — but Ben was extremely hungry and wolfed down his food as his body sent out signals it craved sustenance for the energy burned at hard labor.

The day continued in monotonous regularity until the incident that happened late in the afternoon as Ben was returning with an empty car.

This was the easy part of the job, as the vehicle seemed almost weightless in both its emptiness and the fact it was going down an incline. Ben had just rounded a curve that led into a huge chamber hewn out of the ground during the initial assaults on the earth's coal deposits when several men grabbed him and dragged him off into an uncompleted shaft nearby.

The boy was deposited in front of a burly, tall convict who smiled at him in a kindly way. "What about it, kid?" he asked.

"Huh?" Ben asked. "What about what?"

"Oh, you're a perty'un, you are," the man said. He reached out and stroked Ben's cheek. "Now whattaya say?"

"About what?" Ben asked pulling back. There was

something unnatural and alien about the situation that he couldn't quite figure out.

"I want you to be my gal-boy, kid," the man said. "My name's Morley Jackson." He walked up and put his arm around Ben's waist. "Listen I can get you a soft job down here, like counting the cars. I can get smokes, extry chow, and even candy now and then. Now, c'mon, you want to be ol' Morley's gal-boy, don't you?"

Ben, not at all comprehending the situation but still sensing something strange in the man's tone, turned away. "I got a lotta work to do," he said.

"Well, shit, kid! I'll just let the boys here do what they want," Jackson said. "Then you'll want to be mine."

Ben instinctively slapped at the hands that grabbed him. "You fellers let me be!"

"I can get just about anything anybody'd want here," Jackson said. "Well, not a woman, but that's why I like you. You're so small and cute-like."

One of the other convicts looked over at Jackson who was obviously their leader. "Can we have him now, Morley?"

"Sure," Jackson said smiling. Then he looked at Ben and puckered his mouth in a kissing gesture. "You'll be mine before long, perty li'l gal-boy."

Ben, his mind unable to conceive what was happening, fought as best he could but there were too many. Tears of anger and embarrassment came to his eyes as he felt his pants pulled off.

Ben Cullen came out of the ordeal of his attack shamed, stunned, and almost unable to conceive the reality of the humiliating episode. For two days he ate nothing, simply staring down at his plate while his mental faculties moved along at a tortoise's pace. His mind tried to forget what had happened but was unable to completely submerge the event into nothingness.

Two days later he was once again hauled before Morley Jackson. The older prisoner smiled and put his hand on Ben's shoulder. "What do you say, li'l gal-boy? Ready to be mine now?"

Ben, trembling in rage and fear, said nothing as he tried to back away. But once again, Jackson's henchmen grabbed him and waited impatiently to see what would happen.

"You didn't answer me, perty'un," Jackson said in a soft voice.

"You let me be," Ben said defiantly. Then he swallowed hard. "Please . . ."

"Hold him down, boys," Jackson said coldly. "Looks like I'll have to break him in my way."

Again Ben was overpowered and forced into the act by the larger men. Then, finished, he was shoved away as he groped along the mine shaft for his clothing. He did his best to control his emotions, but now and then a sob escaped.

"Now you think things over, gal-boy," Jackson said with a leer. "You're either gonna belong to ever'body or to me, see? Wouldn't it be nicer to just be one feller's sweetheart, than a whore? Think about it, darling."

By the time he was back in his cell that night, the fright and embarrassment began to subside and a genuine anger eased itself into his consciousness. Just like the uncontrollable loss of temper that had prompted the break-in of the Beardsley store, this new rage prompted him to act.

Ben had noticed the extra pick handles located in a convenient pile at the mine entrance. The constant slamming of the digging instruments against the hard surface of rock and coal caused the handles to split after a few weeks' use. The new ones were kept handy for quick replacement.

Ben waited his opportunity and, at the first chance, slipped one of the brand-new handles onto the top of the push handle of his coal car. He quickly brushed coal dust on it with his hands until it was virtually unnoticeable on the equally filthy vehicle.

That same afternoon Jackson's men were back to fetch him. The largest — and the meanest — of the six men stood grinning as the others blocked the track.

"C'mon, little gal-boy, Morley wants to see you again," the convict said. "And he's real anxious."

"Don't call me gal-boy," Ben said coldly.

"Well, why not, honey, you're the cutest little thing in here," he man said rubbing his crotch.

Ben's cry of rage echoed off the tunnel walls. Adrenaline pumped strength into his skinny arms and the pick handle in his hands was like a flying war club.

The big prisoner's jaw gave way under the blow and one eye popped out of its socket. Ben, still screaming, whirled around in midair and caught the next man in the ribs. The cracking of the broken bones was drowned out by the following victim's bellow as the wooden weapon smashed his testicles.

The others fled.

"I'm a man, goddamn you!" Ben screamed insanely. "You sonofabitches! I'm a man — *a man!*"

It took three guards to bring him under control and

finally drag him, writhing under the kicks and pummeling, out of the mine and back into the prison. They dragged him down to the basement area of the solitary confinement wing and threw him, still shrieking and rampaging, into a bare stone room.

Ben continued the raging fit through convulsions until his voice grew hoarse and he collapsed from exhaustion.

The next day, subdued and quiet, he walked peacefully between two guards who marched him into the captain's office. The senior jailer opened his eyes wide when he saw Ben. "This little feller did all that hisself?" he asked.

"Hell, you shoulda see him, Cap'n," one of the guards said. "Clear outta his goddamned head."

"Musta been," the captain said. He looked at Ben. "How come you done that?"

"I don't know," Ben said.

"Musta been a reason," the captain insisted.

Ben remained silent.

The captain laughed. "Hell, the doc could hardly get ol' Latham's eye back in his head. As it is, it's prob'ly gonna jump out ever'time he sneezes!" The other guards laughed, and their chief continued, "Corwin can't hardly breathe with his ribs stove in like that, and as far as poor ol' Johnson goes—well, I hope to hell he wasn't planning on having a family once he gets out of here."

One of the guards chuckled. "He won't be bothering no more young boys either, will he?"

"He won't be bothering nobody about nothing," the captain said. He looked straight at Ben. "I ain't new to this life, boy. I know what they done, but I gotta hear it from you to make it official. How come you went crazy like that? What'd they do to you?"

Ben said nothing. He was too humiliated and ashamed to admit what Morley and his gang had done to him.

"Well, suit yourself," the captain said. "I got no choice but to give you thirty days in the hole. That means nothing to eat but bread and water. Any comments?"

Ben stared straight ahead.

"Take him down there."

Ben was once again marched away. They took him back to the cell he had occupied the previous twenty-four hours and ushered him in. The guard took a last look at him. "The captain feels pity for you, kid, and some respect too. Otherwise he'd have slapped you in there for six months for what you did."

"I ain't asking nothing from the cap'n," Ben said. "So tell him to give me six months. I don't give a shit."

The guard shook his head. "Boy, you're turning into a real convict at a mighty rapid pace. See you in thirty days."

The cell door slammed shut.

Ben spent those thirty days in silent thought. He lay back on his blanket on the floor — there were no bunks in the solitary cells — and let his mind drift over his short life. All the humiliations and scornful treatment given him by the townspeople of Pleasanton came into sharp, painful focus. The young convict decided then and there that he'd hadn't deserved such scorn. True, his mother hadn't been much and didn't live a life most people approved of, but Ben personally had always tried to play by the rules. He went to school as often as he could and he worked hard at what jobs he had been able to obtain. He admitted to himself that breaking into the Beardsley store had been stupid, and the shame of the deed melted away under the realization that mistreatment and bullying by Oren Beardsley had caused him to do it. He really hadn't bothered Maybelle, except to ask her to dance several times. On each occasion that she'd refused, he'd moved away and kept his distance.

When Ben walked out of the hole at the end of the month, he brought with him a new talent—the ability to hate.

He hated Oren Beardsley, Morley Jackson and his gang, the judge who had sentenced him to prison, the people of Pleasanton, his lawyer, the prosecutor—the world.

The convict population looked on the youngster in a new light now. His action at defending himself elevated him in their crude society. Jackson and his men kept their distance, while the only others to approach him in an attempt to satisfy their sexual urges were newcomers who suddenly had a raging lunatic on their hands. As usual, there would be another vicious attack and Ben Cullen, Convict 2139, would be marched down to the hole for longer and longer stints of solitude, bread, and water.

Ben also became belligerent for other reasons as well. He had frequent fights—most of which he lost—and became a sore spot for the guards. He seemed destined to pull "hard time," making his ten-year term a period of continual conflict and punishments. By his twentieth year, Ben, with four years in the penitentiary, had spent a total of over seven hundred days in the hole.

Then he met Harmon Gilray.

Gilray, serving thirty years for bank and train robberies, had already been in the state prison for three years when Ben Cullen arrived. Several members of his outlaw gang were serving their time with the chief. They formed a hardcore, elite clique that had plenty of outside support and money. While lawyers worked on their cases, they bribed the guards in order to get preferential treatment. When Morley Jackson and his men first picked out Ben to be a girl, Gilray had watched with detached amusement, wondering how long it would be until the youngster would do like all the others and give in. After Ben's first berserk attack and subsequent attitude, Gilray developed a casual interest in the boy. As additional trouble followed, he found out more about the youth. The gang leader, an intelligent and creative but unlettered man, developed an outright admiration for the feisty little prisoner who had seemed to declare a personal war on the Kansas state penal organization. Finally Gilray summoned Ben to his presence. And even a rebel like the slightly built youth knew better than to ignore an invitation from the all-powerful bandit chief.

Ben was ushered into Gilray's spacious cell and stood there looking at the older convict. He saw a tall, rangy man with coal-black hair and dark piercing eyes. His mouth was harsh and thin under the hawkish nose, but Gilray's eyes seemed to dance with a bright light of intelligence and perception.

Gilray smiled easily and offered his hand. "Howdy. My name is Harmon Gilray."

Ben shook hands. "I'm Ben Cullen."

"I called you here because I want to ask you a question," Gilray said.

Ben was curious. "Sure."

"When're you gonna stop being so goddamned mad?"

Ben looked straight into Gilray's eyes for several long seconds. "When hell freezes over."

"Ain't likely to do that," Gilray said.

"And I ain't likely to stop being mad," Ben responded.

"Then, you're gonna die in here, boy," Gilray said. "One day you're gonna run into some sonofabitch that's maybe only half as crazy as you are, and he's gonna knife you or brain you with one o' them pick handles or maybe just pound your ass to a meaty sludge with his fists."

"I reckon that's what'll happen, then," Ben said unemotionally.

"There's something better'n that," Gilray said. "Why don't you take all that mad you got and channel it into something else?"

"Like what?" Ben asked.

"Like making things better for yourself instead of worse," Gilray said.

"In here?" Ben asked incredulously.

"Hell, yes, in here!" Gilray said. "Or out there or even in hell itself. That's the differ'nce between a smart feller and a stupid one. And I think you're smart, Ben Cullen. I been watching you and I figger you could come a long way with a little help."

"You just like being nice to folks, do you?" Ben sneered.

Gilray grinned. "Not unless I got a reason, and I got

a reason where you're concerned, Ben Cullen. Me and the boys can always use an extry hand. And one day all of us is gonna get outta here and back to our old ways. I'd like you join up with me on the outside too."

"Yeah?" Ben was definitely interested. Harmon Gilray's exploits were well known and he was a folk hero of sorts to the convict population.

"But I'm the boss and I make the rules," Gilray said. "So if you want to ride with me, you do things my way. I don't like rebels."

Ben, after four years, had learned to be cagey and mistrustful. "I gotta think it over."

"Sure," Gilray said. "Take your time. I understand you got another six years." He laughed. "That's one thing we all got plenty of, ain't it?"

"How long you in for?" Ben asked.

"Me and the boys got over thirty years on our sentences," Gilray answered. "Which means we oughta be seeing the light o' day around 1908. But, like all fellers that have learnt to be smart, we got things working for us, not *against* us, so we'll probably walk out that front gate before you do. So you go on and give my proposition a little thought. When you decide, just drop by." Gilray laughed. "You'll know where to find me."

"I guess I do," Ben said grinning despite himself. He turned and walked out of the cell, deciding to sleep on the matter that night and get back to Gilray in the morning.

But it was actually two months later.

That evening in the chow hall, Ben became agitated with the man next to him at the table who, crowded like everyone else, accidentally nudged him several times with his elbows. Ben's temper snapped, and once again he was embroiled in a senseless, instinctive attack that ended with another sentence of solitary confinement.

Ben actually felt sheepish when he went back to Gilray's cell. Gilray grinned at him. "I heard you broke a couple of the rules."

"I reckon I did," Ben said with an embarrassed smile. "I'd like to join up with you if the offer's still open."

"It is," Gilray said.

"You can count me in," Ben said.

"You're in, then."

Ben's world changed completely that moment. Within a few days orders were mysteriously issued that moved him into a cell on Gilray's tier. And his job at the coal mine changed too. Instead of earning the $1.23-plus per day as a mine helper, he was reclassified on the payroll as a $1.71½ per day full-fledged miner.

Except he never had to go down into the dark pit and swing a heavy pick at the solid walls of black coal.

He spent his time with Gilray and his men in their own corner of the yard where future bank and railroad robberies, along with intense periods of discussion and instruction in the dangerous profession of banditry, were planned.

The chief amusement of the gang was the competition in knife throwing. As guards looked the other way, the group conducted target practice by throwing the specially honed weapons at boards with crude targets painted on them.

And here Ben Cullen found he had a special talent. After several months, he began winning the games with such regularity that he couldn't find anyone to bet against him unless he offered tremendous odds.

Ben's attitude began to soften somewhat toward the prison life as he enjoyed the best accommodations and food available in the penitentiary as a member of the Gilray Gang. But the hatred still existed unabated in his soul and he now planned to direct that animosity toward society with all the fury he could muster.

Another criminal had been created.

Chapter Five

Ben spent three days outside of Hobart as part of his plan to rob the bank. It was well after midnight on the third night when he rode slowly through the town's streets. Although the moon was bright, it was still difficult to see on the unlighted streets. Ben went to several houses and had to look carefully before he found the one that belonged to W. T. Abernathy, the president of the Kiowa County Bank.

Ben dismounted and went through the gate of the picket fence and up onto the porch. He knocked on the door. "Mr. Abernathy! Mr. Abernathy!"

Finally he could hear the sounds of stirring within the dwelling, and a sleepy but disturbed voice spoke to him through the door. "Uh, yeah, what is it?" Within moments the door opened slightly and Abernathy, his great moustache visible in the moonlight, peered cautiously out on the porch.

Ben, correctly figuring the man had come to the

door armed, stood out where he could easily be seen. "Ned down at the bank asked me to fetch you up to him."

There was immediate concern in Abernathy's voice. "Oh, Lord! What's the matter?"

"I don't know for sure," Ben replied. "He called out to me while I was walking past. He said he'd been waiting for somebody to come by so's he could send him to fetch you."

"He didn't say anything about a robbery, did he?" Abernathy asked.

"He didn't say nothing about nothing," Ben answered. "He just asked me to come by and get you. So here I am."

"I'll let my wife know I'm going down there," Abernathy said.

"You want me to go along with you?" Ben asked in an innocent voice. "Or should I just move on along."

"You might as well go on about—" There was a hesitation. "Are you a friend of Ned's?"

"Yes, sir," Ben said. "We're both working as carpenters. The two of us came to Hobart together."

"In that case it'd be a good idea if you came with me."

"What's your name?"

"John Smith," Ben answered. "I've been in the bank several times on business."

"Oh? Oh, yes, indeed, I remember you," Abernathy said as he vainly tried to recall such a person. "I'll be out directly, Mr. Smith."

"Are you sure you remember me?" Ben put a touch of indignity in his voice.

"Certainly, Mr. Smith," Abernathy said. "I'm sorry, it's just that I'm afraid I'm still quite sleepy."

"I'll wait for you," Ben said.

"Yes, thank you. I won't be long." The door shut and Abernathy's heavy footsteps could be heard going back across the creaking floor of the recently constructed house.

In ten minutes the banker emerged and both men hurried down to the business district with Ben leading his horse. The fugitive, sensing an uneasiness in his companion, began speaking in a calm, reassuring voice. "I just got back from Mountain View. I wanted to be here first thing in the morning to see Mr. Harrison."

"The jeweler?" Abernathy asked.

"Yes, sir," Ben said as his mind fabricated a story. "I'm getting married to a widow lady over there. I plan to buy a nice ring for her."

Abernathy smiled in the darkness as they turned onto Fourth Street off Jefferson. "Well! Congratulations!"

"Thanks," Ben said. "I had my dream of opening up my own carpentry business out here, but I never figgered on getting hitched so quick."

"That's mighty fine," Abernathy said as they walked up to the back door.

"I'll be doing a lot of business with you, Mr. Abernathy," Ben said easing his pistol out of its holster.

Abernathy unlocked the door. "I wonder where Ned is."

As they stepped inside the bank Ben shoved his Colt .45 into the other's back. "Get your damn hands up and do it quick, mister, or I'll put a hole in you they can drive a two-mule team through — wagon and all."

"Oh, my God!" Abernathy exclaimed.

"Just keep your voice down," Ben cautioned him. "I want that safe opened quick."

"I — I left the combination at home," Abernathy said.

"You got ten seconds to have that door swung open or I'm gonna kill you," Ben said in a cold voice. "There ain't gonna be none of this shit of walking back to your house or standing here jawing. I'll make it simple so's you can come up with a quick decision, Abernathy. Open that safe or die!"

"I'll open it! I'll open it!" Abernathy said in fright.

"I told you to keep quiet," Ben again cautioned him. "We'll let ol' Ned snooze through this." He chuckled. "Then you can fire him in the morning when he wakes up and finds you laying here all trussed up."

Abernathy had already turned toward the safe when the simultaneous flash and gunshot exploded aloud.

Ben whirled toward the source of the attack in time to see the gun's brilliant explosion again. This time the bullet whirled so close to his ear he could feel its brief slipstream.

"Get down, Mr. Abernathy!" Ned Brownley yelled. "I'll get him."

Abernathy dove to the floor, but this time it was Ben who fired. Three quick shots barked in the bank, and a groan from Brownley and his stumbling steps showed he'd been hit. Ben turned to look for the banker but couldn't see him in the darkness.

"You sonofabitches!" he yelled in rage.

There was no sense in hanging around hoping to get Abernathy to open the safe now. It wouldn't be long before alarmed citizens would be arriving.

A lot of frustrated bank robbers would have blasted away in the dark hoping to kill the banker in revenge, but cold-blooded murder wasn't Ben Cullen's style. He left the man hiding in the dark and fled outside.

A few lanterns flared up and loud voices could already be heard as Ben leaped into his saddle. He kicked the horse's flanks and galloped madly through the dark streets toward the edge of town as he headed for the open prairie where the moon's light, unhindered by buildings and other man-made structures, would guide him through the night.

During his stay in the Kansas State Penitentiary, Ben Cullen spent a total of three years with Harmon Gilray and his gang.

The organization eventually had its own shack constructed in one corner of the prison yard where they gathered daily for discussions on future plans, bank and train robbery techniques, and the latest news from their outside sources, as well as for general amusement with the ever popular knife-throwing games. Ben firmly established himself as the champion of champions in that event.

During the cold months, with the small wood-burning stove furnished by the bribed captain of guards radiating comforting heat, the group would sit and listen to their gang leader spin his philosophies as he discussed life and sought to slant their views toward his own in an effort to mold them into better outlaws and enemies of society.

"Nobody owns nothing in this world," Harmon Gilray would tell his followers. "They might have something in their possession at any given time, but they're only holding it until a stronger or meaner feller comes along and takes it away. That's why you got to be strong and mean, so's you can have what you want outta life."

"What about nice folks?" Ben once asked him. "Like bankers and such? They got plenty, but they ain't strong or mean."

"Maybe not in a saloon fight," Gilray allowed, "but they're the strongest and meanest, boy. They don't pack guns or knives, but they write laws and papers that make things go their way. Them rules and statutes give 'em the strength they need, and believe me, they're mean enough to see that only the right stuff for them gets passed by the government. It's us poor folks that got to use our guns and fists, boy, that's our law — the Law of the Sixshooter — just like they say in them dime novels. That's one thing them silly magazines have got right."

Sometimes Gilray's preaching confused Ben. But as time went by, his understanding grew.

The outlaw leader even touched on women in his discourses. "The ladies is another problem altogether. They're trouble as sure as hell, and always have been. Remember Eve in the Bible?"

"I sure do," Ben answered. "She give ol' Adam that apple and got him in dutch with God. He was lucky he didn't end up in solitary."

"Solitary is something thought up by men," Gilray said. "Even God never done that to anybody." He paused. "But if the Creator ever did curse men, He done it with women. He give 'em that 'twixt their legs, boy, and if the Lord made anything better'n that He kept it for Himself."

Ben, who had never once in his life gazed between a

woman's legs, only nodded.

"You stay away from 'em as much as you can," Gilray advised him. "If you feel the urge, then pay some dance hall gal for a little of her time, then get on back downstairs with your pards. Don't never go back to the same one again either. And if you ever catch yourself liking one, then get as far away from her as you can."

"I liked a gal once," Ben admitted. "But I reckon I told you about her already."

Gilray laughed. "Yeah. You told us what happened too. Her goddamned brother beat the shit outta you, didn't he? And just on account of what she told him."

"Yeah," Ben said.

"If it weren't for that little gal, you wouldn't be here right now, Ben Cullen," Gilray said, emphasizing his point.

"I reckon not," Ben agreed. "But sometimes I'd like have a gal like me." He smiled. "You know, be my sweetheart or something."

Gilray shook his head at this display of softness. "Are you crazy, young Ben Cullen? In the first place the fickle little bitch is gonna break your damn heart someday and take up with some other jasper. That is, if you're lucky. If you ain't, she'll marry you and make your life a living hell on earth, believe me! Stay away from 'em, Ben. You already got more trouble than you can handle from a gal now, ain't you?"

"Yeah," Ben said. But somehow the thought of having a girl like him seemed like one of the most wonderful things that could ever happen to him. Sometimes, at night in his cell, his active imagination would create scenes between himself and this phantom young woman. These were chaste affairs with affection and tenderness between them. But these pleasant reveries would always drift into jarring, hurting memories of Maybelle Beardsley.

Finally, Ben accepted Gilray's dictum. The man was as right about women as he was everything else.

Chapter Six

Ben's ride out of Hobart had been wild and unplanned. He'd simply headed for the safety of his hidden camp. Now, clutching his Winchester carbine, he knelt in the copse of cottonwood where he'd established a sanctuary.

He had little trouble evading the poorly organized pursuit mounted against him from the town. The posse, who had left late, knew little of the country they searched and they rode in random futility from one end of Kiowa County to the other as Ben lay low in his hiding place.

But suddenly a group of riders, obviously part of the people pursuing him, wandered dangerously close.

One of the riders dismounted and entered the trees a scant few yards from where Ben, all his senses strained and alerted, watched in nervous readiness. The man lowered his trousers and squatted.

"Hey, Hank!" a voice sounded. "Where the hell are you?"

"I'm taking a shit," the man named Hank called

78

back.

"Want something to read?" his companion asked. He followed the question with a cackle.

"Don't take all day," a third man urged him. "Supper's waiting."

"Hell, I figgered we'd catch the jasper that killed Ned Brownley," the man relieving himself said.

Now Ben knew the man he'd shot was dead.

"Yeah," the second pursuer said. "But we don't know this country good enough. Hell, if we was back home in Missouri, I wouldn't have no trouble catching the sonofabitch."

"Yeah," the other agreed.

Hank stood up and readjusted his trousers. "Okay. Let's get on home. We done the best we could."

Ben licked his dry lips and listened as they rode away leaving him sitting alone in the early evening silence. No doubt there would be no more pursuit that day, but he would take no chances. After a couple of hours had passed, Ben carefully checked his camp in the waning light.

He'd learned an important lesson when he first rode the owlhoot trail with Harmon Gilray and his gang: always clean up old camps so no one can tell anybody had even stopped there.

Ben's cookfire had been in a depression he scraped out in the ground. He had piled dirt over the ashes and used dead leaves and grass to cover that in order not to leave even a faint trace of his having been there. Lastly, he took a dead branch and meticulously brushed the area to get rid of tracks he might have left. When he was satisfied the job was done, he swung up in the

79

saddle and, short of cash and supplies, but long on plans for the future, rode north toward the Kansas line.

He traveled slowly and leisurely through the night, letting the horse pick his own way as long as the animal traveled in the right direction. Toward dawn Ben took a two-hour break and caught enough of a nap to take the edge off his weariness and restore some of the energy spent in the last day. Then he continued the journey.

During the late afternoon, over the horizon to the east, a build-up of clouds began. These were black, restless mountains of heavy mist pregnant with moisture and bristling with flashes of angry lightning.

They rolled up higher as they approached in a silent, billowy expansion of celestial majesty while the first discharges of thunder began to roll ominously across the darkening prairie.

Ben could smell the rain and feel the growing coolness as the temperature plunged from the mid-nineties into the high seventies. Within a half hour the entire sky was a rolling canopy of flashing and deep rumbling as the restless, angry cumulus formations edged on in their ponderous but restless trek.

Then the rain hit.

The clouds released their wet cargo in thick sheets of water that measured hundreds of yards across. These descended rapidly from almost two thousand feet and slammed onto the helpless earth like the swat of a giant's hand. Leaves were knocked from trees, birds in flight were crushed to the ground, and the high buffalo grass was beaten to carpet flatness by each successive wave of heavy rain.

Ben reeled in his saddle and even the horse staggered

under the initial watery assault, but finally the weight of the rain decreased markedly until it came in heavy drops. But even these, in the growing wind, obscured all vision as they swept across the prairies in whirling, dancing gusts with enough force to sting unprotected skin.

Ben was virtually blind. He could only hold onto the saddlehorn with one hand and his hat with the other as his mount lurched forward through the storm.

Gullies and dry washes now filled with raging torrents. Many had been river- and creekbeds in ancient days, and were now reverted to their prehistoric state.

Ben's horse, not able to see any better than its rider, stumbled to the edge of a deep cut in the terrain. The slippery, loose mud gave way under the weight of the animal, causing it and the rider to plunge into a brand-new raging river flowing through the ravine where once wild flowers grew.

Ben was swept from the saddle and he swam wildly, almost instinctively, against the current that now rolled and pitched him against the rocky banks. Confused and dazed, he vaguely noticed his boots being swept from his feet as his mouth and nose were filled with the muddy deluge that played with him, bobbing him around like a helpless cork.

He continued to fight the water and grab air as he flailed and kicked. He quickly grew exhausted and his arms and legs seemed to be made of lead. Finally, gagging and hacking, his mind grew dizzy and disoriented to the point he no longer cared.

He sank beneath the flood, all fight gone out of him.

Ben had spent his full ten-year sentence in prison.

Harmon Gilray and his men, through the efforts of their lawyers, finally were released three years before Ben. The outlaw leader left his address—actually his family's farm near Newton, Kansas—and told Ben to look him up after his release.

Ben, now permanently armed with his ever-present knife, found life not so easy without Gilray's presence. He was once again assigned to pushing the coal cars in and out of the mine, but there was only one more sexual attack attempted on him.

This was done by a lone bully who lunged for the youngster one moment and found his belly split open the next. The attacker survived—in maintaining the silence required by prison etiquette and tradition—and Ben was considered a "tough con" by then and not to be trifled with. In the culture of the prison yard he had proved himself a man and was treated with respect from that moment on.

He continued at his job and went through the routine of being a loner. His ever-active imagination made life bearable for him as it conjured up images of dashing bank and train robberies as a member of Gilray's gang. Ben saw visions of money, beautiful women—though he'd yet to have one—and whole dime novels devoted to his life's story just like Jesse James had. This dream world, and the fantasies of hope and grand adventures it created, kept Ben on an even keel. He had the one thing that most convicts didn't have: a dream of a better life than the one he'd had before going into the penitentiary.

A month before his scheduled release, and just a few weeks after his twenty-sixth birthday, Ben was summoned to the prison chaplain's office for an interview.

The clergyman, a tall, thin, severe man named Hamilton, did little to hide the disapproval he felt for his flock. They were sinners of the worst sort as far as he was concerned, and he firmly believed that lawbreakers should humble themselves before him and God—in that order—then spend the rest of their lives crawling before society, begging forgiveness for the crimes that had sent them to prison in the first place.

Ben stood before his desk with the silent passivity he'd learned to display to authority since becoming Convict 2139.

Hamilton had a piece of paper on his desk. "Your name is Benjamin Cullen, is it not?"

"Yes, sir," Ben answered.

"And your prison number is 2139?"

"Yes, sir."

The chaplain held up the piece of paper. "See this? There isn't a mark on it, is there?"

Ben looked at the document. He noted his name at the top and a series of squares covering the remainder. "I see printing, sir," Ben said. "But no marks."

"That's right," the Reverend Mr. Hamilton said as he pursed his lips in indignant disapproval. "This is your chapel attendance record."

"Yes, sir."

"And there's not one indication here that in the ten years you've spent in the Kansas State Penitentiary, that you even once came to services."

"I reckon not, sir," Ben said unemotionally.

"Why not?"

"The folks back in my hometown didn't like me going to their services 'cause I didn't have good clothes or any money to put in the collection plate," Ben said. "So I reckon I never developed much of a habit of attending church."

"Then, no wonder you ended up in here, Benjamin Cullen," Chaplain Hamilton said sharply. "Regular church attendance would have taken you along the right paths in life and steered you away from bad company and evil deeds."

"I always figgered church was for folks from the right part of town, sir," Ben said. "I lived on the other side of the tracks."

Hamilton scowled. "It's true that churches on the outside have no place for riffraff like yourself, Cullen. But that's no excuse not to have gone to chapel here and taken advantage of my counsel and religious teachings."

"Yes, sir."

"There's many things in the scriptures that you could have gleaned during your time here," Hamilton continued.

Ben wondered if the scriptures offered any advice on how a youngster could protect himself from assault by older, larger prisoners, or how to bribe a guard for better food and a warmer cell, or a hundred other things a convict needed to know in order to survive the ordeal of his sentence.

But he said nothing.

"You'll be back here, Benjamin Cullen," Hamilton said with a satisfied grin that showed no humor. "And when you do, I strongly advise you to ally yourself closely with the prison chapel."

"I gotta go, sir."

Hamilton stood up. "You won't go until I dismiss you!"

Ben smiled at him.

"I want you to fully realize that you're a sinner! A damned-to-hell unforgiven sinner who'll burn for eternity," Hamilton said. "You and your kind are like cancers on mankind that must be cut away if you will not be cured."

Ben continued grinning. He had no reason to fear the chaplain. While prisoners up for parole or pardon had to act subservient and humble before the clergyman, others, like Ben, whose sentences were completed could not be affected by any recommendations one way or the other from Hamilton.

"If you won't accept God's will, then Satan will take your soul—"

"Just a minute," Ben said finally speaking. "If I'm bad and that pleases the devil, why in the world would he want to punish me?" This was not an original thought of Ben's. He was echoing one of Harmon Gilray's preachments. "You'd think he'd be pleased as punch with fellers like me."

Hamilton sputtered and could not speak.

"Listen, preacher man," Ben said leaning forward defiantly. "My sentence is up August third, 1891. I'm walking outta here a free man, and there ain't nothing you can do about it. I ain't one of them poor bastards up for parole that's got to listen to your shit and bow and scrape to keep you happy. So piss up a rope, you

85

sonofabitch, I'm gone!"

Ben was returned to his cell and immediately summoned out again. He thought perhaps Hamilton had reported his insubordination and he'd have to spend some time in solitary. But this time the captain of the guards informed Ben he had been removed from all work details and would be moved to a different building where trustees and short-timers were housed.

The new routine made the final month unbearably slow. Ben was locked in his cell and only let out for meals, a two-hour exercise period in the yard, and once a week for a bath. Again he turned to his imagination and began living the the coming days of freedom in his mind as he hoped they would be.

On the final day, Ben went through almost a direct reverse of the admitting procedure. Again he stripped—this time out of the striped prison uniform bearing the number 2139—and he was sprayed with the fire hose. He was marched into the supply room where he turned in his bedding and was given a dusty cardboard box. Upon opening it he found his original clothing. The same suit he had worn to the dance that fateful night ten years previously. No longer a sixteen-year-old boy, Ben found the clothing too small. This was no problem because the state of Kansas provided him with a cheap set of clothing and a shapeless wool army campaign hat that had been dyed a shade of green.

Then he received his earnings from the mine. One hundred dollars in cash for ten years of work except for the time he'd spent lollying around with Harmon Gilray and the boys. But actually he had spent most of his salary buying better work assignments, food, and other benefits put up on the prison market by the guards.

Ben stuck the money in the pockets of the baggy suit, slapped the hat on his head and, on August 3, 1891, stepped out the front gate of the prison a free man.

A guard escorted him to the train station in Leavenworth where he purchased a one-way ticket to Newton, Kansas. Although there was a five-hour wait, Ben had the blue-uniformed official with him right up to the point he stepped up on the train.

Ben, suddenly feeling very frightened and alone, virtually crouched in his seat and watched the wide expanse of the Kansas countryside sweep by his window. He gave his fellow passengers furtive glances now and then until a young woman boarded the train during a stopover in Emporia.

She walked down the aisle with her eyes demurely cast downward as she took a seat in front of Ben. He could see her delicate neck and narrow shoulders, and her hair seemed so soft and delicate to the young man who had been locked up with other males for the previous ten years. There was also a scent about her that caused his heart to beat faster.

A strange longing overtook him. He'd fought down the normal sexual urges that had plagued him in prison. Sex with another man was repugnant and reminded him of the assaults he'd endured. Yet he desired to have some sort of physical relationship with the young woman he now studied so intently. Having her touch him would be heavenly, he thought, even if it were a caress on the face and look into his eyes.

Then he roughly pushed the soft thoughts from his mind. Harmon Gilray would never have approved of them. But looking at the girl did bring him one startling revelation: he could no longer recall what Maybelle Beardsley looked like.

They arrived in Newton early the next morning and Ben was suddenly standing outside alone for the first time in this strange world. People seemed to scurry aimlessly about. There were no groups marching to chow halls or work details or bathouses. No one seemed to have any purpose at all in the senseless activity that went on around him. They came and went, passed by from left to right and right to left, some came at him obliquely while others whisked past him and suddenly turned off into other directions. No one shouted orders or blew whistles to keep things orderly in this hurly-burly of confusion.

Ben was hungry, and suddenly he felt the helplessness of the institutionalized who have to make decisions about things that had been merely part of a former routine. No guard would come along and shove him into a line and take him to the proper place to eat. He had to find it himself.

Ben hadn't read a word in the ten years he'd been in prison. His reading skills, while never particularly high, had sunk to near illiteracy. The lettering on signs and buildings only added to his perplexity. Finally he passed a building in which several men sat at a low counter eating. Ben summoned his courage and walked in and took a seat.

"What'll it be?" a man in a greasy apron asked him.

Ben panicked for a moment. He had to choose some sort of food, but his mind whirled with the effort.

"Hey, you want something or don't you? I ain't got all day," the man asked.

"Gimme some salt pork and beans," Ben said.

"Hell, I ain't got salt pork," the man said laughing. "You like that stuff?"

"Yes," Ben said lamely.

"Why don't you have something I got. Like bacon and eggs?"

"Sure," Ben said secretly glad for the suggestion. "I'd like some bacon and eggs."

"How many eggs?" the man asked.

"Uh—gimme two eggs," Bens aid.

"How do you like 'em?"

"I like 'em just fine," Ben replied.

The cook, exasperated, shook his head. "Looky here now, feller, I'm busy as hell. How do you want them eggs? Scrambled? Fried?"

"Yes, sir."

"How do you want them goddamned eggs?"

"Fry 'em," Ben said.

"Want some coffee too?"

"Yeah," Ben said. "I'd surely like a cup o' coffee, mister."

The cook slapped the meal together quickly and pushed the greasy mess—laid on a dirty plate—in front of Ben. It seemed like a feast of the gods to the ex-convict. "That looks mighty good," Ben said.

The cook, surprised, smiled. "Here's your coffee. Piping hot."

Ben took a sip and sighed in contentment. "That's

89

right good coffee too."

"Well, I'm glad you like it," the cook said. He wasn't used to compliments. "Say, I got an extry piece o' bacon in the skillet. Want it?"

"No, thanks," Ben said suspiciously.

"No charge, feller, I'd have to toss it out anyhow."

Ben was used to gifts being offered for sexual favors. He shook his head again as he wolfed down the food.

"Sure you don't want it?"

Ben, suddenly angry and defensive, finished off the bacon and eggs. He stood up. "How much I owe you?"

"Fifteen cents."

Ben pulled some change out of his pocket and laid it on the counter. "Take it out of there." He watched as the man pulled several of the coins from the pile, then he put the remainder back in his pocket.

"Sure you don't want the bacon, pard?"

Ben's temper boiled over. "You listen to me, you sonofabitch! I'm a man, see? You try any o' your shit on me and I'll cut you three ways—wide, deep, and continuously!"

The cook jumped back in alarm. "What the hell's the matter with you?" he shouted. "Get outta here, you hear? *Get outta here!*"

Ben, glad the man knew he was no gal-boy, grinned viciously at him before abruptly exiting the little cafe.

Ben spent the following two hours simply walking around Newton and looking the town over. The encounter in the cafe made him feel surer of himself now that he had established a reputation in the area. Still displaying the convict's perspective, Ben felt the word of his willingness to fight would pass around quickly making most, if not all, the locals leave him in peace.

Finally he began seeking directions to the Gilray farm. Nobody could help him until he wandered into a barbershop. A farmer getting a haircut offered him a ride out to the place. Ben, feeling secure now, accepted and sat down to wait for the man.

The barber looked closely at Ben. "You want a trim, feller?"

"No, thanks."

"You been having a friend cut your hair?"

Ben, now acutely aware of how his hair must look since being permitted to let it grow out from the prison scalpings, ran his fingers through it. "Yeah. I ain't particular."

"I reckon you ain't," the barber said with a smile. He went back to snipping at the farmer's hair and finally finished.

"Put it on my tab, Harry," the customer said. He got his hat from the rack and motioned to Ben. "Let's go. I gotta pick up my woman and kids, then we'll head on out that-a way." As they stepped outside, the farmer offered his hand. "Elliot Frawley."

Ben shook hands. "Ben Cullen."

"Just outta prison, are you?"

"No," Ben lied.

"It's all right, Cullen," Frawley said. "I done time in Texas. Ol' Harmon Gilray wanted me to team up with him, but I had my family. I can't take no more o' that owlhoot trail."

Ben, suddenly feeling very close and friendly, nodded. "I knowed Harmon up there in the penitentiary. I'm riding with him as soon as I can find him."

"That's what I figgered," Frawley said. He sighed. "Well, it's your choice, I reckon. Ever' man decides his own way to go. It just ain't worth it to me. You ain't got a sweetheart or wife or nothing?"

"Nope," Ben answered.

"Any family?"

"I had a ma, but she died," Ben said. "The county clerk at home wrote the warden and he told me."

"Maybe the choice is best for you," Frawley said. They walked down the street to a heavy farm wagon. A large, square-jawed woman wearing a calico bonnet looked down at them. She smiled. "Who you got there, Elliot?"

"Ben Cullen," Frawley said to his wife. "A friend of the Gilrays. Gonna give him a lift out to their place. Ben, this is my wife, Martha."

"Howdy," Ben said.

Mrs. Frawley nodded and scooted over to make room for him on the seat. "You going to work for the Gilrays?"

"I reckon."

"Nice folks."

"I don't know 'em," Ben said settling down. "I'm a friend of Harmon's.

"Oh." That was all Martha Frawley said.

Like most families on the frontier, the Frawleys were taciturn. Even the kids in the back of the wagon sat quietly as they rolled slowly along the country road. Ben sat there being acutely aware of the woman's presence. Although she was far from being attractive even to him, her closeness and feminity stirred longings in him that he had felt with the younger girl on the train.

Ben, the sexual urges agitating, was glad when the wagon finally stopped. Frawley pointed up a side road. "That-a way. Maybe two miles."

"Thanks," Ben said hopping to the ground. Then, without another word or gesture, he walked away from the wagon toward the farm.

Chapter Seven

The storm had washed the sky clean. Cloudless and a deep blue, it stretched from horizon to horizon with a sparkling clarity to match the sweet, washed smell of the air.

No breezes stirred the stillness of the scene. As was common with prairie thundersqualls, the violent attack had been followed by a placid aftermath. The only sounds were those of meadowlarks, mockingbirds, and a few flitting scissortails that sang as they went about the business of tending their nests and feeding.

Ben Cullen lay face down in a bed of crushed bluebonnet flowers that had been knocked flat by the temporary river that raged over them the previous evening. His clothing was still wet and his damp hair was plastered to his skull. The first stirrings of consciousness caused him to roll over on his back in a reflex to breathe easier. His eyelids flickered against the brightness of the sun that radiated brightly on the scene.

Suddenly his eyes opened and Ben sat up violently.

The effort made him dizzy and he coughed so hard that he vomited up the muddy water he had swallowed during the flash flood. Ben struggled to his feet while every nerve and sensibility of his being tried to scream at him through his mental fog that he was a pursued man and in imminent danger. More dizziness followed and he staggered backward to sit down hard on the ground again.

It took him ten minutes of concentrated effort, but he finally regained a wakeful state. This time he stood up slowly, letting the waves of nausea and vertigo subside slowly before he attempted to move. He checked himself over carefully. He obviously was not injured—there were no pain, cuts, or other signs of wounds—but his pistol was gone from the holster, both boots were missing, and his hat had also disappeared.

He walked around the immediate area searching for his horse and other gear, but could find nothing. He walked up and down the ravine for more than a mile on each side, but the search was useless. He had to accept the fact that he had lost everything. The only weapon he possessed was the faithful knife stuck snugly in the sheath he carried on his back.

Ben's choice of actions was severely limited. He could either sit there and wait for a posse to eventually come along and find him, or he could move along on foot and hope for some wild luck to get him out of the predicament he was now in.

Ben decided to walk.

He went back into the ravine and climbed up on the north side. After a brief determination of which way Wichita might be, he began the trek.

His socks didn't last long. Already worn with holes in

them, it didn't take much time for the rugged terrain to finish the destruction. Ben finally pulled off the remnants and stuck them under a piece of sod he loosened in the ground. As with all men used to being hunted, he wanted to leave no evidence of his passing—not even a worn-out pair of boot stockings—if he could help it.

There were plenty of stickers on the ground, and he had to walk slowly and carefully to avoid getting them stuck in the soles of his feet. More stops were necessary as he sat down to pull out the thorny hunks of vegetation before being able to continue. Although things were bad for him, he realized that he was lucky in a strange way. If a situation like this had happened to some unfortunate traveler twenty years previously, he would have been caught by a wandering band of Kiowas or Comanches. The Indians would have passed the rest of the lazy summer day by treating their victim to a slow, roasting death.

The law was bad enough, but the worst Ben could expect from them would be a quick bullet through the head or a few moments of strangling at the end of a rope thrown over the nearest tree branch.

The morning passed and the afternoon came on with an even hotter sun. The moist earth, baked by the rays, emitted an invisible steam of high humidity. Thirst wasn't too much of a problem, but it couldn't always be slaked in a particularly tasty way because he'd lost his canteen. Ben crossed a few creeks, but most of the water he had to drink was taken from tepid puddles left over from the heavy rain. Still, it helped him to survive and provided the liquid his body required from so much perspiring.

The late afternoon dissolved into early evening as Ben kept up his slow, persistent pace to whatever the fates had in store for him. His feet were swollen by then and his face and hands were badly sunburned. He'd put his kerchief over his head and kept it wet with soakings in the water he found, so he was far from sunstroke.

He spotted a smudge on the horizon. His eyes, tired from the long day in the hot sun, could not be completely trusted, so he would have to avoid whatever the thing was, or make a careful investigation. Not wanting to miss any opportunities to improve his situation, no matter how slim, he decided to check out the unknown thing.

He approached cautiously. Gradually the object of his attention grew plainer in his vision until he recognized it for what it was — an isolated farm.

Ben situated himself on a knoll a half mile from it and studied the setup. There was a house — surprisingly made of lumber rather than sod — and a large barn. The farmyard held a plow and a couple of other smaller agricultural vehicles. That meant there was a horse or mule available there. Even if the animal wasn't particularly swift, it would still be better than no mount.

Then the damned dog started barking.

Whoever was inside would be alerted by then. Ben decided to bluff it out. Playing the role of an innocent traveler badly inconvenienced by the storm seemed a good idea. Particularly since the place was isolated enough that there would have been no news of any fugitives out of Hobart.

There was the problem of the dog, however. If the

animal was vicious, the situation could be serious. Ben reached back and loosened the knife in its sheath. He limped across the broad expanse of prairie and whistled at the dog as he came into the farmyard. Luckily, the hound was friendly and his tail whipped back and forth in joyous greeting. Ben petted him and allowed himself to be sniffed, then turned toward the house.

The door was open and a man stood in it. He stepped out on the rickety porch and waved. "Howdy."

"Howdy," Ben said.

The man indicated the dog with a nod of his head. "Looks like Ol' Bob has taken a liking to you."

"Yeah," Ben said petting the animal again. He walked up to the house and affected a weary smile. "I got caught in the storm yesterday."

The man's face expressed concern. "You sure did, friend. And it appeared that Mother Nature treated you pretty rough. Come on in here."

"I'm a mess. Your floor will—"

"Don't you worry none about that," the farmer said. He held the door open and ushered Ben inside. "I'm Jim Baldwin."

"John Smith," Ben said extending his hand.

"Sit down," Baldwin said offering a chair at the table. "I'll get my missus in here." He went to the door leading into the rest of the house. "Lucille! Lucille! We got comp'ny."

There was a scurry of quick footsteps and not one, but two, women came in. "Who in the world?" They stopped at the sight of the visitor. "Heavens! You must have got caught in that awful storm!"

"Yes'm," Ben said raising politely. "I'm afraid I lost my horse, saddle, gear. Ever'thing I owned on this green earth."

The two women were typical of the type who lived in the open country. Strong, ruddy, with plain faces and wearing their hair drawn back into severe buns, they looked robust and healthy in their plain calico dresses.

"This is my wife, Lucille, and her sister Arlena," Baldwin said.

"I'm John Smith."

Lucille Baldwin hurried to the stove and used a rag to hold onto the coffeepot sitting there. "The first thing you need, Mr. Smith, is a cup of hot coffee."

"I thank you," Ben said. The thought of the stimulant was most welcome.

"We're having a late supper tonight," Mrs. Baldwin said in an apologetic tone. "I hope you don't mind waiting."

"I don't want to be no trouble, ma'am," Ben said. "I'll be moving on after the cup o' java."

"You stay and eat with us," Baldwin said, also getting served a cup of the boiling brew. "We got plenty and you're welcome." He pointed toward Ben's feet. "Besides, you ain't even got boots, Mr. Smith."

Ben knew he really needed the nourishment. One good solid meal like he could get on a family farm would last the skinny outlaw up to three days.

Mrs. Baldwin was as practical as her husband. "Just how much farther do you think you can travel? You ain't got a thing a body needs to get through this wilderness hale and hearty."

The sister-in-law Arlena, who had been quiet, sat down at the table. "We hope you'll stay to supper, Mr. Smith."

"I'm obliged," Ben said in acceptance.

The women busied themselves in preparing the meal. Within a short time the kitchen was filled with the smells of hot grease, frying pork, and boiling beans. Baldwin sat down at the table and the two men sipped more coffee.

"Which way are you headed?" the farmer asked.

"South," Ben said. "I hear there's some new towns opening up down there."

"Sure are," Baldwin remarked. "You got some place in particular to go, or maybe you're just headed in a general direction."

"No place in particular," Ben said. He needed to find out what animals were available, but he didn't want to arouse any suspicion.

"If it's a job you want, well, I got an opening for a hired hand," Baldwin said.

Ben wasn't too surprised at the news. He didn't know too many men who would want to work on a ranch that was so out of the way—except for an outlaw on the run. "I might be inter'sted in working for you, sir."

"All I can offer is found—no cash money."

Ben shrugged. "Mr. Baldwin, I ain't got nothing. Look at me. No boots, no horse, no gear—nothing."

"If you're worried about having to buy something, don't," Baldwin said. "I got a pair of boots—you might have to wrap your feet in rags to make 'em fit, but they'll do."

Mrs. Baldwin turned from the stove. "There was a young feller 'bout your size that used to work for us. He left some stuff when he took off."

Baldwin smiled. "He snuck off with some meat from the smokehouse, so I didn't feel so bad about keeping some of his clothes."

"You don't seem too upset he stole from you," Ben said. "Old outfits ain't worth the cost of meat."

"Don't bother me none," Baldwin said. "If he needed it, he's welcome to it."

Ben was thoughtful for several long minutes. There was no doubt that the Baldwin farm would be perfect for lying low a few days. Not only could he steal a mount, but he'd have some new clothes as well. And Baldwin probably had a rifle and pistols that would come in handy. He hated like hell to think of taking things from these people who were being so good to him, but to not do so would be tantamount to suicide since a hangman's rope was now waiting for him in both Texas and Oklahoma Territory.

"Sure. I'll take the job," Ben finally said.

"Hallelujah! Thank you, Lord!" Baldwin said.

Mrs. Baldwin and her sister raised their hands above their head. "Thank you, Jesus, thank you!"

Ben was puzzled by the reaction.

"We've been praying for weeks to get the help we need," Baldwin explained. "We knew the Lord would come through for us, but we didn't know when or how."

"That's why the storm came last night," Arlena said. "To guide you to our doorstep in this wilderness. Praise the Lord!"

"Yes, ma'am," Ben said, wondering what they'd think if they knew he was a fugitive from the law.

A half hour later the meal was on the table. A platter heaped with pork chops, bowls of pinto beans, and slabs of cold corn bread made up the menu. Before they ate, all bowed their heads and Jim Baldwin offered up a prayer of gratitude.

"We thank you for this bounty, Lord, and ask your

101

blessing on them that eats it. We also thank you kindly for leading our friend John Smith here to help us with the harvest. In Jesus' name we pray. Amen."

"Amen," the ladies said.

Ben ate well. He was offered—and took—thirds of the generous portions spooned out to him. By the end of the meal he was gut-full and stuffed to the limits of his capacity. He could almost feel the extra strength he'd consumed.

Once again there was hot coffee, this time as the ladies cleaned up after the meal. At that particular moment Ben would have liked a few hard sips of liquor, but it had become obvious that Baldwin was more inclined to religion than to drinking. Ben also figured there would be no relaxing game of cards in the evening either.

"Would you care to join us later for our study?" Baldwin asked.

"What kind of study?" Ben asked, puzzled.

"Bible study," Baldwin asked. "We read a few chapters and verses each night, then discuss what they mean to us." He pointed to a shelf where a large Bible sat. "I have some tracts that give us the program to follow. I'm not a real educated man myself."

I don't read," Ben said.

"You'd be welcome to listen, Mr. Smith," Arlena said from the kitchen counter where she was washing plates. "I'm not a real good reader myself."

"Obliged," Ben said, stifling a disgruntled sigh.

Mrs. Baldwin rescued him. "I'm afraid we're being selfish," she said. "Mr. Smith must be plumb tuckered from his ordeal, and here we are talking about keeping him up when the Good Lord above knows he needs rest."

Baldwin clenched his fists in a gesture of self-reproach. "Lord forgive us! You was brung to us, and we're mistreating you something terrible, John."

Ben started to look around to see who "John" was, but luckily remembered that was the name he was using. "Y'all been right nice now," he protested. "I'm fed and feel wonderful. That's a fact."

"There's a nice room out to the barn," Baldwin said. "Them clothes is out there too. I'll bring them boots and a lantern, and you can settle in."

"Are we starting work tomorrow?" Ben asked without enthusiasm.

"Harvest time," Baldwin said as a way of explanation.

The farmer disappeared into the next room and came back with a pair of worn boots. Ben could see right away that they were too big, but Mrs. Baldwin produced some rags from her sewing bag. Ben wrapped them carefully around his feet and tried them on. It was far from a perfect fit, and he would never be able to run or walk far in them, but they would do fine as a temporary fix until something better came along.

"Let's get on out to the barn," Baldwin said. "You can settle in and get a good night's sleep."

Ben followed his new employer out of the house. Arlena went out on the porch with them. "You'll still take all your meals in the house," she said.

"Thank you," Ben said over his shoulder. The dog joined him and walked beside him toward the large outer building.

Baldwin slowed down and let Ben catch up with him. "Arlena is a widow," he explained. "She lost her husband during the trip out here."

"That's too bad," Ben said.

"Yeah, but it was the Lord's will, so there's nothing to be gained by railing about it," Baldwin said, ushering him through the wide barn door.

The sleeping accommodations for hired hands was much more than Ben had expected. He had pictured a crude bunk in one corner of the barn, but there was a separate room. The bed was a secondhand store-bought one with sheets and blankets on the feather mattress. There was a table and chair and pegs on the wall where the former hired hand's clothing still hung.

"Try the stuff on," Baldwin invited him. "He was a young feller, maybe fifteen or sixteen, so his stuff might fit you."

There were three pairs of britches and four shirts. All were patched, but evidently had recently been washed. Ben could picture Mrs. Baldwin and Arlena going to that much trouble in case the thief came back for his belongings. He would have gotten his duds returned along with a dose of forgiveness.

The garments were still a bit loose, but fit well. Any convict at Leavenworth would be glad to have them, Ben thought sardonically. "They'll do fine."

"Good," Baldwin said. "There's a wash basin on the stand there, and the well is in the yard. I'll see you in the morning—bright and early."

"Bright and early," Ben said. "Good night."

"Sleep well, friend Smith," Baldwin said. "And may the Good Lord give you peaceful dreams."

"Thanks," Ben said. He didn't bother to get under the covers. Instead he prepared the clothing he'd inherited into a handy bundle for a quick getaway, then settled down for the night on the bed after blowing out the lantern.

The night passed with its usual fitfulness for Ben Cullen. He awoke many times to listen for strange or unfriendly noises before dozing off again for a quick cat nap. He even got up a couple of times and walked around the barn. Old Bob the dog happily accompanied him, licking at his hand to beg for some petting.

Dawn was only a pink hint on the horizon when Baldwin appeared at the door of the room. "John," he called. "John Smith." He knocked on the door.

Ben sat up. "C'mon in, Mr. Baldwin."

Baldwin stepped inside. "I see you're dressed already."

"I guess I fell asleep with my clothes on," Ben said, standing up. "We ready to start work?"

Baldwin laughed. "How about some breakfast first? We got fresh eggs and some of that cornbread left."

"I'd be partial to some coffee," Ben said going out the door with his employer.

"We got that too," Baldwin promised.

Both women were in the kitchen. Arlena displayed a wide smile for Ben. "How do, Mr. Smith."

"Morning," Ben said. "That coffee smells good."

"I made it myself. "I don't use the beans more'n twice," Arlena said. "Some folks might consider that a waste and a sin, but I think good, strong coffee is mighty important. Let me get you a cup."

"I'm obliged, ma'am," Ben said, sitting down at the table.

The meal was as good as supper. And, like that repast, began with a prayer from Jim Baldwin.

"Lord, we thank you for this bounty and ask you to

bless them that eats it. We also ask your blessing on this day's work. In the name of Jesus we pray. Amen."

"Amen," the women said.

The eggs were plentiful and scrambled. The thick hunks of corn bread had been heated on top of the stove. Ben shoveled it in with a gusto that seemed to please both Mrs. Baldwin and Arlena. Even Baldwin was happy. "I like to see a man partake hungrily of what the Lord provides, John," he said. "A strong appetite shows a clean heart and soul."

Ben smiled to himself on hearing the last remark. But he went on eating until he'd cleaned up his plate for the third time.

Jim Baldwin stood up. "You know how to use a scythe, John?"

"Yes, sir. I sure do," Ben answered.

Baldwin smiled. "I got one that ought to fit your hands, then."

Ben also got to his feet. "Then, let's go harvest some wheat."

Mrs. Baldwin looked heavenward. "Praise the Lord! We've got the help we prayed for. There's no doubt."

"Not a bit," Baldwin said.

"Thanks to Jesus!" Arlena said.

All the religious remarks made Ben feel a bit uneasy. He had never been treated as a deliverance from God before.

The farmer and the fugitive went out to the barn to get their tools for the day's work. The walk to Baldwin's small wheat field was not long, so within a quarter of an hour Ben was lost in the rhythm of swinging the scythe back and forth as he progressed up and down the field.

Even though Ben's mind was lost in the monotonous regularity of the task, his eyes wandered to the distant horizons often. He felt positively naked without as much as a small-caliber derringer. The only thing he had was his faithful knife. The most he could hope to do would be to cut down one adversary before the others would blast him to mincemeat.

He and Baldwin stopped after several scything trips up and down the grain-filled meadow, going back and tying up the wheat into shocks to ready them to be picked up and tossed into the back of the wagon before being taken back to the barn. Their work was only interrupted when Arlena showed up with a fresh bucket of cold well water. The woman always had time to chat a bit with Ben before going back to the house.

After one such break in the toil, Baldwin grinned over at Ben. "I think Arlena has taken a shine to you."

"Naw," Ben said. "I don't think so."

"She's a widder-woman, Ben," Baldwin said. "And a young'un at that." Then he added, "She don't have no kids neither. They died in the same epidemic with her man Tom."

"That's too bad," Ben said. "Did you and your missus lose your young'uns that way?"

"The Lord has decided we're not to have any children," Baldwin said a bit sadly. "Me and Lucille accept it, though we're disappointed."

"Too bad," Ben said.

He went back to his work, completely lost in it except for occasional worried glances out at the surrounding countryside. The labor was hard in the hot weather, and the reddening glow of sunset was a welcome sight to both men. They trudged slowly back to the house for a big supper that Lucille and Arlena had toiled over most of that day.

Baldwin was obviously pleased with Ben. After the meal, he pushed his plate away and glanced over at his hired hand. "You done a day's work and that's a fact."

"Glad to earn my keep," Ben said. His arms were already aching from the heavy toil. He slurped down the last of his coffee. "If y'all don't mind, I'd like to get a little fresh air. It's kinda close in the house after being outside all day."

"It sure is," Baldwin agreed.

"Mind if I join you, Mr. Smith?" Arlena asked. "I could use a breath myself."

Ben was a bit surprised at the boldness of the woman. "Don't mind a bit," he replied politely.

The two stood outside, looking off into the deep prairie darkness. Arlena stood close to him. "Jim is certainly pleased with your work, Mr. Smith. I can't ever recall hear him saying such a thing to a hired man before."

"I'm glad to help you folks out."

"You was most certainly an answer to our prayers," she said. "The Good Lord sent you to us, and that's a fact."

Ben smiled at the thought. "Well, I'm glad to be here one way or the other."

"Are you really, Mr. Smith? This farm is so far from ever'thing."

"It's a right nice place," he assured her.

"Did you like the peach pie?" Arlena asked.

"I truly did."

She lowered her eyes modestly. "I made it."

"You're a good cook all right," Ben allowed.

"I've been told that," she said, "but I don't know if it's true or not."

"Oh, it's true, ma'am. Believe me," Ben said sincerely.

"I do love to cook and that's a fact."

Ben nodded, his sharp eyes sweeping the open countryside for any signs of movement that didn't belong there.

Chapter Eight

The sun streamed into the hired hand's room in the barn. Ben stood at the washstand, shaving in the cracked mirror mounted on the wall. This was something else he had inherited from the former hand. The straight razor had hardly been used, attesting to the light beard of its former young owner.

Ben was refreshed and wide awake. In fact, he felt positively coltish and energetic. It seemed that for the past several years there had always been a haze of fatigue hanging over him that was only whisked away by occasional periods of sheer panic. But a combination of hard physical labor and the tranquil environment of the farm had caused the outlaw to accomplish something he hadn't done of a long, long time.

He had slept through the entire night.

Ben actually couldn't remember how long it had been since he'd enjoyed such luxury. The deep, dreamless sleep that had so engulfed him took him far away from the fears and troubles of his conscious world.

Ben dressed hurriedly, wondering why Jim Baldwin

hadn't awakened him for work as he had done all that week. Then Ben remembered it was Sunday. Jim had told him the night before that it was a day of rest, according to the Scriptures, and would be so observed.

He walked out of the room and found Ol' Bob the dog waiting for him with wagging tail. Ben petted him fondly, then walked across the barnyard to the house. Mrs. Baldwin stepped out on the porch to empty a basin of dishwater. "Good morning to you, Ben."

"Good morning, ma'am," Ben said. "I think I over-slept."

"You deserve to after all that hard work you've done," Mrs. Baldwin said.

"Good morning, Ben." Arlena leaned out of the kitchen door.

"Morning, Arlena," Ben replied.

"We already ate, but I saved you some," Arlena said.

Mrs. Baldwin laughed. "Jim was going out there to wake you up, but Arlena wouldn't let him."

"I don't mind warming you something," Arlena said. "Come on in the kitchen."

"Obliged," Ben said. He did as he'd been invited and sat down to a hot cup of coffee at the table. As he watched Arlena hustle up some food, Ben felt different. Not so much from hours of refreshing sleep, but mostly from a feeling of peacefulness that had been gradually growing on him while living with the family.

There had been no turmoil since the time he'd arrived. Everything was in apple-pie order, with a sedate routine of hard work and good meals. Ben had experienced no conflicts, no spasms of fear or flashes of his bad temper. He'd been treated with more than respect; there had been a great deal of kindness

111

extended his way. His idea of stealing Jim Baldwin's horse and guns was now completely abandoned. Ben Cullen could not rob the Baldwins under any circumstances—not even to save his own neck from a hanging. Somehow, those people had touched him—down, down deep in his soul—and tickled a part of him that had lain dormant for more than twenty years. Ben decided he would do the greatest thing in the world that he could possibly do for the good family.

He would get the hell out of their lives.

Arlena put the plate in front of him. The eggs and fried potatoes smelled delicious. "We're having services this morning," she said.

"Services?" Ben asked between bites.

"Jim is a lay preacher," Arlena explained. She got a cup of coffee for herself and joined him. "The folks in the area always come of a Sunday to hear him preach."

The feeling of tranquility vanished in an instant. "What folks?"

"Other farmers," Arlena said. "Actually, it ain't ever' Sunday. Only once ever' three or four weeks. It's kinda hard for most folks to get here, since there ain't any roads or anything, and they're spread out so far."

Ben now wished he hadn't stayed. But there was little he could do at that point except hope for the best. He relaxed as he realized that possibilities of them hearing of a fugitive in the area were rather remote. But, still, there was always a chance.

Ben finished his meal and went outside after promising to attend the worship with Arlena.

It was a bare half hour later that the first people showed up. It was a large family with eight kids in a heavy wagon. The woman shouted a happy greeting to

Mrs. Baldwin and produced a large basket of food. Within a half hour other conveyances appeared bearing farm families. The other women arriving also had brought eats that were put in the general larder.

Ben gritted his teeth and kept in the background as much as possible. Jim Baldwin introduced him to a couple of the men, but the fugitive avoided spending prolonged time with any particular individual. He moved around as much as possible, and even disappeared into his room at times when it was feasible.

When the services began, Ben stood in the rear of the throng who had situated themselves on the various buggies and wagons that had brought them there. Arlena quickly joined him. "You like the backs of crowds, huh?"

"Yeah," Ben said weakly. "I don't feel so put upon that way."

"Me too," Arlena said. She looked up into his face. "Jim likes folks to hold hands during services. Would you hold mine?"

Ben displayed a crooked smile. "Pleasure, Arlena."

Arlena gripped his hand and pulled it in close to her.

Jim Baldwin's pulpit was as simple and rustic as the people who stood before it. There was only a farm wagon, but he took his place on the seat as if he were preaching in a grand cathedral. He looked down on his flock.

"It's so good to see you folks again this Sunday. Praise God, you all could make it."

"Praise the Lord!" came a chorus of shouts.

"I hope you've all enjoyed the bountiful blessing of the Lord," Baldwin said. "I know we have. As you all know, we've been in a real hurt without hired help since that boy took off. I can tell you we had some mighty hard prayer sessions, and the Lord in Heaven answered us by sending John Smith to us. He's standing back there with my sister-in-law Arlena. Some of you have already met him, but the others will have a chance after the services. Hallelujah! He's a good worker too, neighbors."

There were some cries of happy congratulations, and several people waved at Ben. He made a slight nod to the greetings, feeling nervous. Arlena's smile was wide and happy, and she gave his hand a little squeeze.

Baldwin began the services with an opening prayer, then called for a couple of hymns. There were no hymnals in the congregation, but they knew the songs by heart. Men, women, and kids made up for any lack of musical sophistication with the gusto and gut feelings they put into the joyous songs praising their Maker.

After the final hymn, Jim Baldwin began his sermon. It was a simple message delivered to plain folk by one of their own who felt he had been called by God to minister to the small flock.

"Folks," Jim began. "I want to talk to y'all about forgiveness. It's something we talk about ever'time we say the Lord's Prayer. We ask Him to forgive us as we forgive them that trespasses agin' us. But, folks, it's one thing to mouth them words, and another to practice 'em."

"Amen!" somebody shouted.

"I know it's hard out here where they ain't no law to back up a man," Jim went on. "If somebody takes something from you, there ain't no way he's gonna be punished unless you—maybe with some neighbors—go

114

after the jasper and get aholt of him yourself."

Ben knew the feeling of the man being chased.

"Now, I allow as to how that ain't wrong when you do it to get something back. If a feller steals a harness you need outta your barn, why, just chase him down and get it back. If you have a mind, then tell him how wrong it is of him to do it and let him know what an all-fired inconvenience he's made. But, folks, the Lord then wants you to forgive him—*forgive* and *forget*—that's the Lord's way. Don't whup him or mistreat the poor sinner. Give him the Word of the Lord, then turn him a-loose."

Ben remembered what Jim had said about the hired hand who had stolen the meat from the smokehouse. He'd said if the man needed it, he was welcomed to it. Evidently, Jim Baldwin literally practiced what he preached.

"If you let the feller go on his way, you might open his eyes to the Lord's ways, folks. Mercy and goodness hits harder'n meanness and revenge any time. I want you to remember that. And the next time we say the Lord's Prayer, and you get to the part about forgiving your trespassers, give it some extra thought. I'd personally appreciate it, and the Lord will be most pleased."

"Praise God!" one of the worshippers hollered fervently.

"Yes, brother, Glory to Him on the Highest!" Jim said. "Now let's jump into 'Rock of Ages,' and let our sweet Lord in Heaven know how much we worship Him."

The hymn was sung joyfully and with great emotion by the small congregation. Several closed their eyes

115

and raised their hands above their heads as if each word of the old song created a special, deep rapport between themselves and God.

It ended and there were several moments of satisfied silence. Jim Baldwin held his Bible, and gestured at the crowd. "And, now, folks—"

"Hallelujah! Hallelujah!"

A tall, lean farmer with a weathered, lined face walked slowly from the crowd and approached the lay preacher.

"It's Fred Loomis!" someone yelled.

Loomis stopped in front of Jim; he looked up at him with tears streaming down his face. Jim leaned down over him, almost shaking with emotion. "What is it you want here, Fred Loomis?"

"Oh, Jim. I come to find Jesus."

"Glory hallelujah!" Jim shouted aloud. He raised his Bible and shouted to the sky. "We thank you, Sweet Lord, for bringing our strayed brother to us." He turned back to the other farmer who was now down on his knees. "Say it again, Fred Loomis! Praise God! Say it again!"

"I come for Jesus!" Loomis shouted.

Jim Baldwin leaped down from the wagon. He gripped one of Loomis's shoulders and began praying aloud.

Ben in the back of the crowd stayed silent. He was acutely aware of Arlena's hand gripping his. There was also something about the services that gnawed at his gut. It was a feeling of discomfort, regret, and yet there was a soothing side to it too. Whatever emotions it brought out in him, it was more than Ben Cullen could stand.

Arlena sensed the surge of emotion. "Do you feel it, John Smith?"

"Huh?"

"Do you feel Jesus a-calling you? Listen! Listen! He's a calling to you, John," Arlena said. "He wants to save you."

"I, uh, I reckon I don't hear nothing," Ben said.

But Arlena was not discouraged. She put her free hand on his arm while making her grip on his hand even tighter. "You'll hear Him soon, I know! That's why He sent you here to us, John."

"Well, maybe so," Ben said. He breathed in deeply to regain control of his tossing emotions.

This was the religion of his people — stark, unabashed, and as wide open as the country they lived in. This sort of worship appealed to them with its simplicity, openness, and the promise that their trials and hardships during their short mortal journey across the face of the earth were only temporary. Religion pledged that something better lay ahead than fourteen hours of hard toil under a broiling sun, death from unknown sicknesses, and the cruel uncertainty of weather during the growing seasons.

Ben finally regained complete control again. He now had the world and his plans back in the proper perspective. He was more interested in survival and avoidance of death by hanging than in seeking the Kingdom of God. Religion was for honest, hardworking farmers — not for a man wanted for murder.

The services continued in unrestrained joy. The saved man, Fred Loomis, was feted and hugged with plenty of pats on the back as he was welcomed into the congregation. Arlena took Ben around by the arm and

117

introduced him to each and every person present. Her mannerisms were those of a woman with her man, and Ben had to admit she sure as hell wasn't the shyest woman he had ever met.

The meal was a huge feast. Every farm woman seemed to have tried to outdo the other in both the quantity and quality of the food she brought to the services. Ben, whose lifestyle dictated that a man eat as much as he could possibly hold at every opportunity since there would be plenty of hungry times in between, flattered and pleased the ladies with his appetite. Their most common expression at seeing him devour their food was: "I love to see a hungry man eat!"

Summer afternoons and evenings are long on the prairie, but most of the people had a great distances to travel. Sunset was still hours away when the crowd broke up. Empty pots and dishes were repacked into baskets for trips homeward, and farewells made among people who had no regular contact with each other. The main attraction of the day was Fred Loomis, who still received best wishes — and also several shopping lists. He had business in Red Rock, a town some distance away that was too far for all but the most necessary of visits.

Ben was glad to see the visitors depart. The peaceful feelings he had been enjoying before the services returned as the last buggy rolled out of sight over the horizon.

Jim Baldwin stood beside him, patting his belly. "I reckon there won't be a need for supper tonight."

"I reckon," Ben agreed. "I think I ate enough to last me a week or two."

Baldwin laughed loudly. "I'll tell you one thing, John

118

Smith. You can sure put the vittles away." They turned and walked back toward the house. "Well, this is the most peaceable time o' the week for us, John. Sunday evenings is time to sit on the porch and sort of relax away what's built up over the previous seven days. We'd be most pleased if you'd join us."

"I'd be happy to," Ben said.

The four people sat in silence mostly. Sunsets are as prolonged and lovely on the wide horizons of prairie country as they are on a quiet evening at sea. There are no mountains or forests to break up the distant lines of land, and the sun takes its time as it sinks and colors the sky at the same time.

The moon was also bright that night. The sky had a few high clouds that obscured nothing. It was as easy to see across the farmyard as if it was high noon. Ben stretched, then finished off the cup of coffee that Arlena had fetched for him. "I reckon I'll turn in."

"Me too," Baldwin said. "We got threshing tomorrow."

Ben stood up. "G'night."

"G'night."

He walked across the yard to the barn and went inside. After sitting down on the bed, he pulled off his boots Baldwin had loaned him, and unwrapped the rags he used to help the fit. The footwear worked fine that way, and he hadn't gotten a blister or suffered too much discomfort. He stood up and took off his shirt, then lay down on the bed with his pants on.

"John."

Ben quickly sat up. He could plainly see Arlena standing just inside the door of his room. "Yeah?"

"John, you're a man — and I been married before, so

I know men," Arlena said.

Puzzled, Ben continued to look at the woman, curious to hear what her visit was about.

"I know what men want, John," Arlena said. She slowly began to unbutton the top buttons of her calico dress. She opened it to reveal her breasts, large and protruding in the moonlight. Then, just as languidly, she refastened the garment. "I am a Christian woman, John Smith. And if you want me, you'll have to marry me."

"Uh, yeah."

She abruptly left him.

Ben lay back down on the bed. He stared at the ceiling in thoughtful silence for a while. No woman had ever offered herself to him like that before. Plenty of cowtown whores had made themselves available for a price, but this was the first time Ben had experienced such a thing where affection and commitment were included. His present situation and the previous ten years of his life prohibited any thoughts of settling down, so there was no reason to torment himself with useless dreams of happiness with any woman.

Ben closed his eyes and drifted off to sleep.

That night he was restless again. Ben figured it was because of the strangers who had come to the services. He awoke several times, and even went for a walk with Ol' Bob. When Jim Baldwin came for him in the morning, Ben was wide awake. He followed him into the house for breakfast.

Arlena served his food, brushing lightly against him from time to time. And from the way Mrs. Baldwin checked out her performance, it was plain to see that the whole idea was something both women had cooked up. Baldwin himself didn't seem to be aware of what was going on.

"Threshing is a terrible hard thing," he said. "You'd better dig into that food, John."

Arlena smiled at Ben. "At least you won't have to go out in the field. You'll be working right close-by."

"Mmmm," Ben acknowledged with a mouthful of food.

The wheat they had scythed and shocked had been brought in on the wagon. It was stacked in the barn, ready to be laid out and flailed to separate the grain from the husk. When that had been done, and it was sacked up, Jim Baldwin would take it all the way to Red Rock in order to sell and barter it away for the things they needed at the general store there.

The men started the work immediately after breakfast. It was unpleasant in the barn. Dust and chaff filled the hot air, and the labor itself was muscle-cramping hard. They used flails and beat down on the wheat in uneven rhythms, the staccato out of tempo but loud.

To Ben it was like digging coal in the penitentiary. A man learns to let his mind go numb and not pay attention to the burning fatigue as he works with the mechanical concentration of a machine. Up-and-down-up-and-down, walking in a circle around the stalks with Jim Baldwin opposite him.

There was no talking. Just occasional grunts as the whack-whacking went on through the morning. The passage of time meant nothing to the men concentrating on the difficult, monotonous task. They were surprised when Lucille Baldwin called to them.

"Dinner!"

121

They dropped the flails without speaking and trooped over to the trough. Ol' Bob, excited, scampered along with them hoping that at least one of them would finally give him some attention. But the two workers simply scooped up water and poured it over themselves. Arlena appeared with soap and towels, and they washed away the grimy, musky smell of male sweat and dried off. "Lucille wants to see you," Arlena said to Jim.

"I hope she don't want wood chopped for the supper fire," Baldwin said. "See you at the table, John."

"Right," Ben said.

Arlena picked up the towels they had draped over the trough. She had undone her top button and leaned over to expose cleavage. When she was sure Ben was watching, she continued for a few more moments then stood up. Her voice was soft and friendly. "You look tired."

"I am."

"It's too bad you won't have a woman for comforting you tonight, John Smith." She smiled coquettishly. "Jim will be all tuckered out like you from all this hard work, but Lucille knows how to give him some nice refreshments."

Ben smiled. "They seem a happy couple."

"A happy man is one with a woman," Arlena said. She leaned over again to pick up the soap. "It's a natural way to be, and he gets a lot more'n just good food, John Smith."

"I reckon he does."

"It's a reward God gives married men."

"And a mighty good'un too," Ben remarked.

"Well," Arlena said. "Let's go up to the house. I'll give

you the onliest thing I can—something good to eat."

"That'll be fine," Ben said.

When they arrived at the kitchen, Jim Baldwin was making an exasperated gesture. "You called me in here special to tell me what we're having for supper?"

Lucille smiled at Arlena as she spoke to her husband. "I just thought you might be inter'sted."

"O' course I am," Baldwin said. "But I didn't have to cut my washing up short to come in here and find out now. You coulda told me while we was eating dinner."

"I guess I'm just a silly woman," Lucille said. She looked over at Ben and Arlena. "Well! Let's sit down to dinner."

They all bowed their heads while Jim Baldwin prayed, "We thank you, Lord, for this bounty and ask you to bless them that eats it. We also thank you for the wheat you give us. In Jesus' name. Amen."

"Amen."

The work was immediately resumed after the meal, and went on until nearly dark that evening. Baldwin's wheat crop was typical for a homestead of that size, and produced a half dozen bushels. The final chore was to sew the bags shut with heavy twine then carry them up to the second floor of the barn. Baldwin had a special platform constructed there to hold the prize crop. The support poles of the device were heavily greased to prevent field mice and other rodents from reaching the grain.

"That's done," Baldwin said when the final bag was lifted into place. "We'll have a late supper, John, but a most welcome one."

"You bet," Ben said.

The meal was a talkative one despite the heavy

fatigue that bore down on the men. The next day's labor would be light now. There was some harness mending, and a bit of fixing up of the barn. Although winter was months away, there was always the chance of an early one in which the white hell of a howling blizzard would descend on them from the north with the same unexpected ferocity of the storm that had wiped out Ben's belongings.

The two men went out on the porch after supper. They sat on the steps and made small talk for a while. Ben would have practically given his right arm for a good smoke and a bottle of liquor, but he still couldn't complain much. A bellyful of good food was nothing to take too lightly.

"We ain't really settled matters on the job here, John," Baldwin said looking over at him. "Have you give any thought about what you're gonna be doing?"

"Not really," Ben answered truthfully. He felt he was in a limbo, but realized that he was going to have to make a move soon.

"This job is permanent if you want it that way," Baldwin said. "There ain't much to do in the winter . . ." He laughed. "—O' course, I don't pay much either, do I?"

"Things is fine around here," Ben said.

"Arlena really likes you," Baldwin said. He let it hang, not pushing it.

"She's a fine woman," Ben said. After a few moments, he stood up. "I'm hitting the hay. Today tuckered me."

Baldwin also got up. "Me too, John. I'll see you in the morning. G'night." He went in the house.

Ben walked across the farmyard, then suddenly

stopped and walked back. He went up on the front porch and knocked on the door.

Baldwin, his wife, and sister-in-law were still in the kitchen. "What is it, John?" the farmer asked.

"I'll be leaving in the morning," Ben said.

Chapter Nine

When young Ben Cullens got out of Leavenworth and joined Harmon Gilray and his boys on the farm near Newton, Kansas, he found he'd arrived at a very good time.

The gang had been taking it easy for a few months. Before that they'd preyed on trains to the north in Nebraska, the Dakotas, and on into Montana. The success they'd enjoyed paid off handsomely, but it also attracted considerable attention to themselves. The railroads had gone all out to catch them. Squads of private detectives and bounty hunters combed the countryside making things so hot that Gilray had led his band back south to friendlier territory.

Serious discussions and planning was under way to leave their sanctuary when Ben showed up at the front door. He'd walked two miles up the road from the place where the farmer named Elliot Frawley had dropped him off.

Ben could see the farmhouse from the road and he cut across a plowed field to get to it. An old woman, smoking a pipe, was shelling peas on the porch. She'd watched the stranger approach without displaying too much interest. If Ben had been on horseback, or with several others, she would have whistled a warning. But the small man approaching seemed relatively harmless. Still, she was suspicious.

Ben stopped at the edge of the porch. He took off his hat. "Howdy, ma'am."

She said nothing, only waiting for him to speak again.

"I'd like to see Harmon—Harmon Gilray—if he's to home," Ben said.

"Harmon don't live here. He ain't here." There was a definite finality in the tone of her voice.

"Yes'm." Ben took a breath. "He said I should come here."

"When did he tell you that?" she asked.

"Up to Leavenworth."

The woman suddenly laughed. "I shoulda knowed when I seen that silly ol' green hat you got. All the boys was wearing 'em when they got out."

Ben grinned, embarrassed. "Well, ma'am. That's what they give us."

The old woman took her pipe out of her mouth and emitted a piercing whistle that echoed across the distant prairie. Seconds later the front door opened and a man stepped out. He wore a full beard, and his hair was in bad need of trimming. He glanced over at Ben. "Damn my eyes! Ben Cullen!"

Ben could barely recognize the greeter. The last time he'd seen him his hair was clipped short and he was clean-shaven. "Is that you, Hog Turpin?"

"It sure is!" Turpin said. He jumped down off the porch and clapped Ben hard on the shoulder. "C'mon in, you, Ben Cullen. Ol' Harmon is gonna be plumb tickled to see you."

Ben nodded to the woman as he crossed the porch. "I thank you kindly, ma'am."

She laughed again. "Them hats is the silliest looking things!"

The reunion was resplendent with more handclasps, shoulder smacks, and happy whooping. Harmon Gilray looked even leaner and tougher than he had in prison. He sported a large moustache, but his hair was still cropped short — though not in the same style as in Leavenworth. "By God, Ben Cullen, I'm glad you showed up. You're just in time for another foray."

A bottle of bourbon was brought out and passed from man to man among the eight there. The last drinking Ben had done with them had been raisin jack, the homemade stuff made on the illicit still they had erected in their shack in the prison yard. Harmon Gilray was curious about one thing. "How many more days of solitary did you pull after we left?" he asked.

"Oh, I took a coupla trips to the hole," Ben admitted. "But not as many as I would have if I hadn't listened to you."

"You need my guiding hand, Ben Cullen," Gilray said.

"I sure do," Ben said sincerely.

Besides the old gang, there was one more man. He was about the same age as Ben, and was named Elmer Woods. Elmer had been in jail in Missouri a couple of times, and was cousin to one of the gang members. He and Ben were destined to hit it off right away, and a fast friendship would be formed between the young outlaws.

"We're gonna have a night o' celebrating before we ride out on the owlhoot trail," Harmon said. "It's kinda hard to find a place to kick up your heels with the law right on top of you."

Elmer Woods added, "And it's hard to find a gal that'll let you too close after you been living out in the woods and prairie without bathing too reg'larly"

"That's the worst part," Hog Turpin said. Ben remembered him as being the one who'd talked the most about women and sex while they were in the penitentiary. "I just can't stay away from whores for too long a spell."

Harmon Gilray winked at Ben. "We're goin' someplace tonight that oughta really inter'st a feller outta jail, Ben." He paused. "Unless you done dipped yore wick in some whore."

Ben shook his head. "I come straight here," he said. "As a matter o' fact this here likker is the first I had since I walked out that front gate."

There were yelps and teasing. "How long has it

129

been since you had a woman, Ben?" somebody asked.

Ben, who was a virgin, didn't want to lie outright to his friends, so he simply said, "I been in prison for ten years, boys."

More whooping followed and Gilray motioned toward the door. "Let's get saddles on them horses and take ol' Ben on down to big Nell's. This boy needs him a woman!"

The place Gilray referred to was a whorehouse east of Newton. A former stage station, it had been rebuilt with a second floor added and the saloon area expanded. The rustic pleasure palace was run by a large woman who kept a stable of acceptable women and a bar stocked with fairly good whiskey. The prices weren't cheap, but that was because she was forced to share her profits with some of the local law.

Ben was issued a roan by the gang. The grayish-yellow horse had been a bonus taken from an unlucky railroad detective who had given his life for the Union Pacific. Ben had never rode much before prison, and the ten years spent there had all but wiped out any equestrian skills he'd possessed in the past. Ben provided some more laughs as he took a couple of falls, but his new friend Elmer Woods kept close-by and urged him back into the saddle with shouts of encouragement.

By the time they reached Big Nell's, Ben was bruised a bit, but not in too bad a shape. The gang stormed in and received a greeting from Big Nell herself. The madam stood six feet tall and weighed in excess of two hundred pounds. Though well groomed, she was a trifle overdressed, but had a friendliness about her that made her a good operator in the profession she had chosen to follow.

"Nell!" Harmon shouted with his arm around her large waist, "We want some good whiskey, then I want you to get a special gal for my ol' pard Ben there."

Nell reached out and grabbed Ben, pulling him violently to her large bosom. "He's a cute li'l feller, Harmon. But any o' my gals will do. They all special."

"No! No!" Gilray insisted with a wag of his finger. "I mean special—*special*! This boy has just been released from prison. Ask him how long he was in there."

Nell looked down on Ben with genuine sympathy. "How long was you up there, boy?"

"Ten years, ma'am."

"Ten years!" she shrieked.

"Yes, ma'am."

"Wanda! Wanda!" Big Nell yelled. "C'mon over here."

A dark-haired, thin young woman with large breasts sauntered over with a whore's smile on her painted face. She knew she'd been picked out for the small fellow with Nell's enormous arm around him, so she played it up to the hilt. She swayed her hips and wet her lips, letting him drink it all in. She wore a thin robe, and the outline of her body showed through it even in the weak lantern-light. She spoke

131

to Nell, but her eyes were on Ben. "What can I do for you, Nell?"

"You got to help this feller out," Nell said, loosing her arm.

"Sure thing, and it's my pleasure to spend some time with this handsome jasper," Wanda said. She slipped her own arm around Ben.

Harmon Gilray and the boys yelled and whistled. Elmer Woods leaned toward the whore. "Turn him inside out, Wanda!"

Wanda winked at Elmer. "You know what I can do, big boy."

More yelling emphasized her boast.

"Wanda, honey," Big Nell said. "This is special with — what's your name, honey?"

"Ben, ma'am."

"Yeah. This is special with Ben. He's been in jail for ten years, so you take him upstairs and do what you do best."

Wanda leaned her face close to Ben's. "I know where you itch, big boy, and I got just what you need to scratch it." She took his hand and led him to the flight of stairs. They paused and Wanda waved to the crowd before ascending to the second floor with Ben trailing obediently behind her.

They went into the room with Ben's head spinning. He had never had a woman, but he had some natural desires that were feeding his instincts with the information he needed. The urges he felt when he'd been close to the girl on the train and sitting beside the farmer's wife on the ride out to the Gilray farm were nothing in comparison with the way his blood pounded in his head at that particular moment.

Wanda was more of a pragmatist than a seducer despite her talk and promises in the bar. She wasted no time in shucking her robe and getting on the bed. Ben numbly stripped down to his longjohns, and stared down at the woman who lay before him with spread legs.

This was sex—and sex was a dirty, humiliating thing that happened when younger, smaller, weaker men were preyed on by those stronger. It was painful and detestful. But the principal thing that bothered him was that she would not be willing to perform the deed if she wasn't paid for it. The situation was too much like a convict giving something to a gal-boy for a quick coupling.

Although Ben looked at a woman, he remembered Morley Jackson's prison gang and all the other rapists at Leavenworth.

"What's the matter, big boy?" Wanda asked. "Can't get it up?" She smiled and beckoned him to join her on the bed. As he complied, she began applying her whore's skills. "Something the matter, hon?"

Ben was mortified, but he felt no urges. Things had been fine until it was time to commit the act. But the thought of having sex with the paid woman was downright disgusting. "I don't know," was all he could say. "I don't know."

But Wanda was sympathetic. "Listen to me, big boy. You been in jail for ten years. Hell! That ol' john-peter o' yours can't remember what to do."

"Shit," Ben said miserably.

"Hey, big boy," Wanda said, getting up and slipping back into her robe. "Don't you worry none, huh?" She winked at him. "And we'll tell them pards o' your'n that you inned me and outed me like a damn stud bull."

"But when you're randy again, you spend your money here on me," she added. "Or I'll tell 'em you don't like women, hear?"

Ben nodded.

"Now gimme five dollars extry and I'll put on a show for your damn friends," Wanda said.

Ben's expression was somber. "Sure."

When they got downstairs, Wanda complained to Big Nell of how tired she was after Ben. She wailed about wanting the next three days off while Harmon Gilray and the boys cheered.

"C'mon, Ben Cullen," his new friend Elmer Woods said. "I'm gonna buy a drink for a man with a pile-driving ass like yours."

Ben, his red face interpreted as self-consciousness, was led to the bar to finish out the evening in a long, yelling, shit-kicking drunken binge. The only sober moments were when he would suddenly remember his failure upstairs. He tried to brighten his mood by remembering what Wanda had said about him needing time to get back to normal.

But it was never to be.

Two days later, the gang rode south to a rendezvous with two more men in the Kiowa country of the Indian Territory. This duo, who had also been in

134

prison at Leavenworth, had been on a special scouting expedition to check out a bank in a small town in New Mexico. The institution was reputed to hold a large amount belonging to the local cattlemen's association. This money was regularly kept there for a brief period in late summer each year after the end of the season for rounding up and selling the herds.

The entire raid involved nearly two weeks in the saddle, but it was well worth it. The bank was hit on an afternoon, and not a shot had been fired as the gang made a clean getaway back to Indian Territory. It was on this trip, during a stopover in Texas, when Ben was first introduced to Paco Chavez and his wife Florita. Ben was to see the Mexican many times over the ensuing ten years that followed.

His friendship with Elmer Woods was also strengthened. Elmer, surprisingly, was the son of a Baptist minister. He'd taken plenty of teasing as a youngster as a "preacher's kid." Anxious to prove he was even wilder than the other boys, he embarked on a series of petty crimes. After a couple of warnings from the local judge, he was packed off to the Missouri State Reformatory for a solid year. He came out of that experience a sworn enemy of society, and spent six months on a rampage that led to five more years behind bars. Elmer went west after his discharge from custody to join his cousin in Kansas who had also just been released from confinement. This was Wes Woods, one of Gilray's men, and Elmer soon became accepted as a full-fledged member of the organization.

The New Mexico bank job netted Ben two thousand dollars. He spent it with the others over in the Cherokee nation. A couple of more trips to whorehouses proved once and for all that the experience in Leavenworth had left him impotent and unable to perform sexually. It was ironic that Harmon Gilray still railed at him about never getting attached to a single woman.

The gang continued to prosper. Banks and trains fell before their guns, and they even became braggadocios, leaving calling cards and notes daring the law to catch up with them. They lived on a seesaw of financial success, either having plenty to spend or nothing at all. They gave the future no thought, only living the present for all it was worth, and Ben Cullen loved it.

As usual, Gilray sent men ahead to pick out their next jobs, and it was Elmer and Wes Woods who returned from Dallas, Texas, with information on a bank that was begging to be hit by the gang. They even brought sketch maps of the street layout, and Harmon Gilray settled down to make careful plans.

But, despite the minute and detailed organization for the job, it was to be the beginning chords of their swan song.

The problem for the Gilray gang was that they spent too much time in the wild country. Untutored and self-educated at best, this isolation kept them ignorant of facts they should have known. Even Harmon Gilray, though he was a cunning and intelligent man, did not fully realize or appreciate the fact that Dallas was a city. There would be no hick sheriff with a couple of deputies to face there. Instead there was a small but well organized police department that worked three shifts around the clock. When there was trouble at night, no one had to go wake up a sleepy town marshal at his home.

But much of their self-confidence and cockiness was badly shaken when they rode into the commercial area past the large Neiman-Marcus retail store. However, the Texas Southwest Bank sat there on the corner per the sketch map, and not one of the outlaws would betray his nervousness with suggestions to call off the robbery.

The attempt was a disaster from the start. Armed guards in the bank were the first to react. This was an ill-trained, poorly paid pair of ancient gunmen long past their prime. Their reaction to the sudden appearance of a half dozen masked men in the lobby was to open fire quickly and effectively.

Two bandits and three customers fell in the hail of lead. The return fire failed to hit the guards. Both, being experienced old hands, had leaped behind the counter with the tellers after their first fusillade.

When the firing broke out, Ben Cullen and Elmer Woods were out in the street holding the horses. A couple of city policemen who had been only a block away showed up quickly and cut loose on the two young men outside. Ben and Elmer fired wildly and inaccurately as Gilray led the other three survivors out of the bank and to the horses.

A wild gallop out of town followed. It would take a

while before a pursuit could be mounted, so Gilray took complete advantage of the time to keep his men moving northward at a rapid pace. They finally slowed enough to keep from killing their horses, but their flight continued on north through the evening. After holing up during the hours of darkness, the gang was again on the run at first light. They didn't stop until late that same day when Gilray led them into a small ranch yard a few miles north of Terral, Oklahoma Territory.

There was a husband, wife, and a teen-aged daughter at home. The gang was to learn that there were two sons also in the family, but they were north in the Creek Nation on a horse-buying errand. Gilray showed a streak of meanness in dealing with the rancher. Ben was upset the way he shoved the man around and bullied him, but rationalized that this was a desperate situation that called for some extreme measures.

But the incident with the girl was something else.

Hog Turpin was a randy son of a bitch. He went to Big Nell's outside of Newton more than any of the others. The weeks on the trail had left him sexually frustrated, and the sight of the girl, who possibly was around fifteen years of age, aroused him. He waited for his chance to get her. It happened while everyone else was in the house. She had to tend the evening milking of the cow and Gilray had detailed Hog to accompany her during the chore to make sure she didn't run away.

Hog would have gotten away with it if he'd managed to keep his hand over her mouth, but he slipped in his excitement and she let out a yell that aroused the others. Her father would have braved the guns of the outlaws to save his daughter, but his wife pleaded tearfully with him to let the men take care of the situation.

Ben was the first on the scene. What he saw sickened him. It was something he, too, had experienced in prison and his rage was no less than it had been during the assaults he'd had to endure. He drew his Colt and brought the heavy pistol down hard on the back of Hog's head.

The attacker bellowed in painful rage and rolled off. This gave the girl a chance to gather up her clothes and run to the house, but it didn't do Ben any good at all. Hog launched an enraged attack against the younger and smaller outlaw. Ben fought hard against the larger man, but in the end was given a bad beating that left him with one eye a bright purple and swollen shut, a broken nose, and a gash over the other eye.

Elmer Woods tried to help Ben, but only got a solid punch to the jaw and a kick in the groin for his troubles. A couple of the others pulled him out of the fracas and held on to him.

Harmon finally pushed Hog away and made him go back with the others. The gang leader looked down at Ben and slowly shook his head. "You ain't got a lick o' sense sometimes, Ben Cullen."

"You all right, Ben?" Elmer asked.

"Shit, yeah. I was just whupped," Ben said. "This

ain't the first time and won't be the last either."

Gilray gave Elmer a shove. "Get your damn ass back to the house, pronto!"

Elmer was defiant. "You want me to stay, Ben?"

Ben shook his head. "Ever'thing is fine now. I'll see you later."

Elmer looked him over carefully before leaving him and Gilray alone.

Ben was still unbowed despite the defeat. "He didn't have no right—"

"Right? He had all the right in the world," Gilray said. "A man has to take what he wants. That's what this ol' world is all about. The onliest thing you gotta do is be a man and back up your pards."

"He was hurting her," Ben said slowly, getting up. "The girl ain't as strong as Hog. There wasn't nothing she could do but put up with it unless somebody helped her." He recalled the other convicts looking away while he was attacked in prison. Many times Ben thought he hated them worse than the rapists.

"It wouldn't have been no big thing for her to let ol' Hog have a good time," Gilray said, disgusted. "Hell, boy, I know why it riles you so. It's because o' what happened to you in prison. But it ain't the same."

"Why not?" Ben snapped back. "It seems to me it's the very same."

"No it ain't, on account o' that's what she's gonna do anyhow when she gets married or has a sweetheart," Gilray argued. "Hell, you ain't no gal-boy that likes other men to do things to him. That's why you fought back so hard there in Leavenworth."

But Ben was unconvinced. "It was still wrong," he said, wiping at his bleeding nose as he walked back to the house.

Hog Turpin didn't seem to hold a grudge over the incident, but it wouldn't have mattered if he had.

The gang's next job was their last. They tried to rob a train west of Little Rock, Arkansas. Railroad detectives were present in the coaches as well as in the baggage car. Hog Turpin and the others died — so did Harmon Gilray.

The gang leader screamed his rage as he was shot from the saddle. He staggered to his feet and returned fire until the barrage from the private policemen blew away half his skull and turned his torso into ground meat.

Elmer Woods took two hits. One, not so serious, tore away a large hunk of flesh from his waist. The other hit his shoulder and went inward and down. Ben, unhurt, moved fast and got them both out of the area while the cadavers of the rest of the gang bounced grotesquely on the ground under the thunderous fusillades pumped into them.

It was lucky the railroad detectives had no horses to chase them, because Ben and Elmer had to travel slow. Elmer recovered a couple of times, but each relapse was worse than the other. Finally, on the outskirts of Fort Smith, Arkansas, he slipped from his saddle, and Ben could not help him remount.

Elmer Woods was dying.

There was absolutely no way he could survive his

gunshot wounds without medical attention. Ben sat with him, giving him the only comfort he could. That was by dipping his bandanna in the creek that flowed past their resting spot and wiping at his pardner's feverish brow.

Elmer awoke and became lucid nearly twelve long hours after his previous collapse. He spoke faintly to Ben, weakly patting him on the arm. "Go on, pal. There ain't nothing left to be did for me."

Ben forced a crooked smile. "Aw, hell, Elmer. You'll be right as rain in another day or two. Then we'll head for the Kiowa country or go see ol' Paco."

Elmer slowly shook his head. "I just can't do no more, Ben."

"That ain't so," Ben said, again bathing his friend's face.

The two lapsed into silence and Ben did some heavy thinking. There were two clear choices: abandon Elmer and get on back to the Indian Territory and safety, or take a terrible chance and try to get him to a doctor in Fort Smith.

Ben gritted his teeth and made the decision.

Late that night he helped Elmer onto his horse and took him slowly and carefully into the town. There were few people about, and Ben stopped one citizen who appeared to be returning home after a considerable amount of time in a saloon.

"Howdy," Ben said.

The man, bleary-eyed and staggering, stopped. "Why, now a howdy to you too." The drunk swayed as he looked at Elmer up in the saddle. "Hey. What's

142

a'matter with 'im, huh?"

"His horse threw him and stomped him," Ben said. "We need a doctor bad. Can you tell me where there's one."

"Sure, sure, sure," the man said. He turned and spun completely around. "Wait a minute." He repeated the motion, this time slowly and carefully. Then he pointed. "Straight down there is a doctor with a shingle out on his porch. Y'can't miss it."

"Thanks, mister," Ben said. He grabbed the reins and gently led Elmer down the street.

The drunk had been accurate in spite of his condition. There was a house on the edge of the commercial district with a sign that advertised a medical doctor in attendance. Ben helped Elmer down and half dragged and half carried him to the porch. "This here's a doctor, Elmer. He'll help you."

Elmer swallowed. "This here's Fort Smith, ain't it?"

"Sure is," Ben said.

"You know who lives here? Judge Parker."

"Isaac Parker the Hanging Judge?" Ben asked.

"Yep," Elmer said with a note of relieved resignation in his voice. "That's who this doc is going fix me up for."

"Damn, Elmer!"

"Don't worry, Ben," Elmer said. "You done right by me. There never was a better pard." He grinned with a grimace. "We'll meet again in hell."

"So long, Elmer," Ben said. "Good luck."

"Good luck to you, Ben Cullen.

Ben banged on the door until he could hear some

143

stirring inside. Then he raced to the street and mounted his horse. The young outlaw turned toward the Arkansas River and rode toward it. The sanctity of the Indian Territory was over on the far bank.

Chapter Ten

Ben Cullen's last breakfast on the Baldwin farm was a somber affair despite Jim Baldwin's attempt to keep the mood at a high level.

Ben knew it wouldn't be a happy meal, so he tried to leave without bothering the family. He also could not bear the thought of awkward good-byes. All Ben wanted was to make an unannounced departure and simply walk away before dawn. But both Lucille and Arlena had gotten up early that day to prepare a good meal and were bustling around in the kitchen. While Lucille prepared breakfast, Arlena worked on packing a lunch for Ben to take with him.

Ben had just left the barn and was walking toward the farmyard gate when Lucille saw him from the kitchen window. She ran outside and called to him, "John! John! Don't you go yet!"

He hesitated. "It's all right, Mrs. Baldwin. I don't

want to be no trouble."

Arlena appeared beside her sister. "John Smith, you get right inside this kitchen. I fixed up a nice lunch for you to take along and I won't let it go to waste."

"O' course." Lucille said. "And you need a hearty meal if you're off on a long trip, John."

"Obliged," Ben mumbled. He was torn between two feelings. He really wanted to get moving, but the thought of beginning the next phase of his journey on a full stomach was appealing too. So was the opportunity to spend a bit more time with Arlena.

He went inside. Jim Baldwin was already having a cup of coffee at the kitchen table. "Howdy, John. You didn't think we'd let you get away on an empty belly, did you?"

Ben grinned. "I shoulda knowed better." He sat down. "I really appreciate this."

"It's the least we coulda did after all the hard work you been doing for us," Baldwin said.

The two men sat in awkward silence for the next ten minutes. Finally the meal was served and the ladies seated themselves. They all bowed their heads.

"Lord," said Baldwin, "we thank you for this bounty and ask you to bless them that eats it. We also would like to ask you for an extra blessing on John here. He's off on a long journey and we've growed fond of him. We'd be most obliged if you look after him. In Christ's name we pray. Amen."

"Amen."

No one said anything for the first few minutes of the breakfast. Until, finally, Lucille spoke up. "My! Aren't we a gloomy bunch? C'mon, ever'body, we're starting another wonderful day that the Lord has give us."

"I guess we should rejoice in that," Baldwin said. The farmer took a bite of his fried potatoes and glanced across the table. His voice had a forced cheerfulness in it. "Well, John. You have any solid plans or are you just going to drift with the wind?"

Ben's scheme to get to Chicago via Wichita, Kansas, was till very much in effect. But he wanted to throw as much smoke across his trail as he could. "Oh, I got some serious ideas," he said. "I guess I told you I was inter'sted in the new settlements to the south. There's good opportunities for a feller that wants fresh country to start out in."

Arlena, who hadn't said a word at all since coming in from the porch, finally spoke. Her voice was low and her eyes were downcast to her plate. "A wife'd be as handy there as anywhere," she said.

"I reckon," Ben agreed. He'd spent a sleepless night, taking a couple of walks with the dog, as his mind worked out all that he must do if his run for freedom were to successfully continue. In addition to those perplexing and serious problems he had under consideration, there was another source of mental turmoil that kept interfering with his thought processes.

Ben Cullen was in love with Arlena.

He'd fully realized that the previous evening before he'd left the family to go out to the barn. It was the reason for his abrupt return to the house and announcement of his departure. Ben's affections and considerations were absolutely sincere. He cared enough for the woman to put her happiness and well-being ahead of his own selfish desires, but the worst thing that could happen to the woman would be to find herself deeply involved with him.

Another reason for his wakeful night had been the physical evidence that he would be completely capable of making love to Arlena. His body had ached and throbbed for her. Ben knew that any sexual intercourse would be shared experience and an expression of affection between them. All the old barriers, born in prison, were swept away with the realization. He lusted for her, but in a most tender way. Despite these carnal drives, he stifled his physical longings out of love for Arlena.

Lucille went to the stove and returned with the skillet of scrambled eggs she was keeping warm to one side of the hot grill. She spooned out another generous portion on Ben's plate. "A traveling man has got to build up his strength, John."

"Obliged," Ben said. He was in bad need of a horse and firearms. It would have been so easy to have taken care of those problems in the dark of the night, but Ben could not commit any wrongdoings against this family.

"I hope you'll let me borry these boots," Ben said to Baldwin. "I should've asked, but I figgered it was all right."

"It sure is, but you'll keep them boots," Jim Baldwin said. "And the clothes that was out in the barn."

"Arlena washed 'em, and I bundled 'em up for you," Lucille said. "There's even a rope sling so's you can carry 'em on your shoulder."

"I'll send you money," Ben said.

But Baldwin shook his head. "You more'n earned 'em, my friend John Smith."

148

When they finished eating there was an awkward silence. Ben glanced across the table to take in one more sweet glimpse of the woman he loved. Any more delay would only increase the pain in his heart. He suddenly stood up. "I'll take my leave now."

They all got to their feet and went with him through the door and out onto the porch. Ben shook hands with Baldwin, then with the two women. He thrilled to the feel of Arlena on his flesh even if it was only her hand. Ben knew that the memory of her standing in the barn, her bare breasts showing in the moonlight, would be the sweetest of his life.

"So long," Ben said. He picked up the bundle and slung it across his shoulders. after stepping down onto the ground, he began walking across the farmyard in rapid strides.

He'd reached the gate when he heard Arlena's voice shouting.

"John! John!"

Ben stopped and looked back. The woman was running toward him from the house. As she drew nearer, he could see the tears on her face. "Yes, Arlena?"

Arlena ran up to him and stopped. She was so out of breath she could hardly speak. When she finally did, her voice was broken with sobbing. "Oh, John! What's the matter with you?"

He ached inwardly, knowing for sure now that she loved him too. "I just got to go. That's all, Arlena."

"Why? Why?" she demanded tearfully.

He slowly shook his head. "I got to. It can't be helped."

149

"Don't you want nobody to love you, John?" she asked. "Are you a-scared to have that happen? Just stop now, and let me reach out to you and take you and hold you, John. Please!"

"It just can't be."

"I love you, John, she said, crying. "You got to let me want you and cherish you. Why won't you?"

Ben knew he might even start bawling himself if he didn't leave. "I'm doing it out of consideration for you," he flatly stated. After one more look, he quickly turned and walked away. After a minute he stopped and looked back. Arlena was back at the gate, her head down as she wept. He gazed at her, and when he spoke he did so in a tone so low that Arlena could never have heard him even if she'd been a lot closer. But he said the words he'd never said to another human being before in his whole life:

"I love you."

The three mounted men came over the crest of the hill at the same moment he resumed his journey. The unexpected sight startled him, stirring up the feelings of anger and fear that had been dormant those past few weeks. Ben glanced wildly around, looking for someplace or something to help him get away.

But there was nothing.

They were lawmen, they were armed, and they had those guns trained on him. The middle man, wearing a sheriff's badge, reined up. "Is your name Ben Cullen?"

Ben shook his head. "My name is John Smith."

One of the deputies, the tallest, sneered at him. "The hell it is! We got a poster on you in Red Rock. You answer the description perfect, you little sawed-off runt."

"Get your damn hands up!" the sheriff suddenly yelled as he realized that Ben was simply standing there. "Or you're a dead man, Cullen. You won't do to us like you done that marshal, I swear to God!"

Ben raised his hands and could hear Arlena, Jim, and Lucille rushing up to where they all stood.

"What's the matter, Sheriff?" Baldwin demanded.

"Is this the man that's been working for you?" the sheriff asked.

"Sure," Baldwin said. "And he's a good worker too."

"We heard about him from that farmer Loomis," the lawman said. "He was visiting my deputy here and saw the poster on Cullen. He said he seen a man that looked like him during church services over here a couple o' weeks back."

Now Ben knew he should have left that same day.

"His name is John Smith and I can vouch for his honesty," Baldwin said.

"He's a fine man," Arlena insisted. "He come to us as an answer to our prayers."

The sheriff was blunt. "His name is Ben Cullen and he's wanted for murdering a deputy U.S. marshal over in Texas, and for killing a bank guard down in Hobart." He glared a Ben. "Only God knows what other things he's done and ain't got caught at."

Arlena's voice trembled with anger. "John couldn't have did things like that!"

The other deputy, who had said nothing, was more businesslike. He dismounted and came up behind Ben. He roughly pulled his hands down behind him and locked on a set of handcuffs. "You got a hell of a walk ahead o' you, Cullen. All the way into Red Rock."

"Wait!" Baldwin interrupted. "I'll get my wagon and let him ride."

"Are you crazy?" the sheriff asked. He motioned to his deputies. "Let's get moving."

A rope was placed around Ben's neck and tied off to the tall deputy's saddlehorn. Humiliated and in bonds, he was led away in disgrace from the family — and the woman — he had learned to love.

The local lockup in Red Rock was crude and incredibly dirty. The poor ventilation made the cells sweltering sweatboxes. This particular discomfort brought back memories of Leavenworth to Ben. As he sat on the bunk, he could remember the thirst and sweat in the cells there on hot summer evenings after spending the days laboring in the hell of the coal mine.

He had been locked up there for three days waiting for the deputy marshals from Guthrie to come over and pick him up. The sheriff hadn't fed him until the second evening, and all he'd had that third day was a cup of water.

The door to the cell block opened and the taller deputy stepped inside. His name was Denton and he did nothing to hide his hatred of Ben. He grinned. "I was just checking up on you."

"I ain't gone no place," Ben aid.

"Well, now, don't you worry none about that if you still got a hankering to travel," Denton said. "You'll be heading over to the territorial prison to get hung. You'll get a trial first in Guthrie, o' course. But the end result is as good as decided. You don't shoot down two good men and get away with it, Cullen."

Ben realized that the lawman wasn't aware that one of the men he was charged with killing had died from a knife wound. And that same knife still rested in the sheath on his back. The small-town sheriff had not searched him beyond his pockets.

Denton leaned against the wall. "I wonder what it's like to be hung, Cullen." He cackled loudly. "They say your neck just breaks"—he snapped his fingers.—"like that. But I bet you feel it."

"Could be," Cullen said. "When you get down to hell, look me up and I'll let you know."

"I'll sure do that," Denton said.

"And you can tell me how it felt to die from being so damned stupid."

Denton's temper snapped. "You want me to come in that cell and stomp you good?"

That was exactly what Ben wanted him to do. The knife was ready and all he'd have to do would be to grab it and flick the blade into Denton's body. But, unless the cell door was opened, it would do him no good. Ben poised himself on the edge of the bunk. "You couldn't whip me, Denton. Not on your best day."

"You little sonofabitch! If it weren't for getting in dutch with the sheriff, I'd teach you a good lesson before they hung you."

"C'mon, Denton. Just try it." Ben stood up.

"You shitass," Denton said. He went back to the cellblock door and opened it, then glanced back at the prisoner. "Looks like you got visitors, Cullen. That dirt farmer pal o' your'n and them women has just stopped outside."

He went to the outer office. Ben could hear the sound of voices and recognized Jim Baldwin's, Lucille's and Arlena's. He hoped the deputy would come get him, but the door opened again and the family came into the cell area.

"Whew! It's sure close in here," Baldwin said. "Howdy, John."

"My name is Ben," he replied. "Ben Cullen."

Lucille smiled. "It seems funny to call you that after all the weeks you was 'John' to us."

Ben took a deep breath. "I'm sorry I lied to you about that. And I gotta tell you too. I'm wanted for murder like the sheriff said. And I—"

"Shush!" Arlena said. "Just shush. You don't have to say nothing or explain nothing."

Baldwin nodded his agreement. "She's right. All this is part o' the Lord's work."

Arlena stepped forward and smiled fondly at him. "I brung you a basket."

Denton, who had been standing behind them, pushed through and took the food from the woman. "Pris'ners ain't allowed gifts," he said, " 'specially murdering little runts."

Baldwin's voice was calm, but his eyes betrayed his anger. "I'll thank you, please, not to insult our friend. He's already locked up, what more do you want to do to him?"

"How about hanging him?" Denton said. "I'll take the basket outside and you can have it back when you leave."

Arlena walked to the bars. "We prayed for you last

154

night, John—I mean, Ben."

"I ain't worth it," Ben said.

"Yes! Yes, you are," Baldwin said. "You're on your way to a new beginning, Ben."

"I'm on my way to get hung," Ben said.

"No," Lucille said, "Jim sat up all last night and listened to the Lord. He can do that, Ben. He's had the Call."

"The Lord has forgive you, Ben," Baldwin said. "That's why He sent you to us. It was His way of having you start over. We know you're a good man, Ben, we seen you what you are inside while we was living with you."

Ben was more pragmatic about the situation. "If God wanted me to start over, how come he sent them lawmen after him? Or should I say, how come he let the jasper named Loomis tell the law where I was?"

"I don't know," Baldwin said. "The Lord does things in a way that us poor ol' mortal men can never understand. But, listen to me, Ben. You ain't gonna be hung."

Arlena's face radiated. "The Lord has let him know that. You'll be coming home soon."

"The Lord told you I was getting loose?" Ben asked.

"We told you before," Arlena said. "Jim's had the Call."

Baldwin smiled. "It ain't like when you and me talk, Ben. God revealed it to me while I was reading my Bible and trying to figger all this out."

"I hope you're right," Ben said.

"Ben, I know you ain't a real religious man," Baldwin said. "But would you pray with us?"

"Please!" Arlena begged.

"Sure," Ben said.

"Let's join hands," Baldwin said.

Arlena reached through the cell and grabbed Ben's hand. Her touch was comforting to him. He reached out with his other and grasped Lucille's. Baldwin stood between the two women. The small group of people bowed their heads.

"Lord," Baldwin began, "you servant Ben is here in jail now. That's what you wanted, though we can't figure out why. We all believe in you, Lord, and I know that Ben is coming to Christ soon now. We'll bide our time and wait for your Word. But, God, could we ask you hurry things up a little? Forgive our impatience, it's just that we learned to love ol' Ben so much. In Christ's name we pray. Amen."

"Amen."

"I feel so much better now," Lucille said.

"Oh, and I do too," Arlena said smiling. She gazed into Ben's eyes. "What about you, Ben?"

He forced a weak smile. "I feel fine."

"There's one thing you gotta do, though," Baldwin said. "I know it's necessary before the Lord will move on with whatever he's got planned for you, Ben."

"What's that?" Ben asked.

"You got to forgive Brother Loomis for turning you in," Baldwin said.

Ben shrugged. "Sure."

"Say it, Ben! Say it!" Baldwin urged him.

"I forgive ol' Loomis for turning me in," Ben said. He really didn't much care about Loomis one way or the other. When things bad happened, they just happened as far as Ben was concerned. There was no sense in carrying a grudge.

"Do you mean it in your heart?" Baldwin asked.

Ben nodded. "Yeah."

"Praise the Lord!" Arlena exclaimed, clasping her hands together.

"Glory!" Baldwin said. "Glory to God on the highest!"

Denton stepped back into the cellblock. "Time's up. Let's go."

"Couldn't we stay longer?" Baldwin asked.

"Yes," Arlena begged. "We come so far."

"Can't do it," Denton said with a tone of finality. "The sheriff's rules is got to be obeyed."

"We'll pray for you, Ben," Baldwin said. "And you'll be delivered soon."

Denton smirked. "He'll be delivered, all right. Straight to the hangman at the territorial prison."

"Obliged for your visit," Ben said. "It was truly nice."

"Good-bye, Ben," Arlena said. "We'll see you soon."

Ben leaned against the bars and waved at her. Everyone left and the door closed, leaving him alone. Ben walked back to the bunk and sat down again.

He was happy that he had done nothing wrong to the Baldwin family.

Dusk was gathering and the shadows across the cell floor lengthened as Ben lethargically watched their slow progress. He was hungry, but that was nothing new to him. He'd learned to endure it long ago. Being hungry was part of his life, like cold in the winter and heat in the summer.

The door opened and both the sheriff and Denton appeared. The deputy had a tray with him. "We got to feed you, Cullen," he said. "I'd feel real bad if you starved to death before you got to your necktie party."

"Stay there on the bunk," the sheriff warned him as he approached the cell door. He stuck the large key in the lock and pushed it open. "C'mon, Denton. Don't stand there all night."

"Sure," Denton said. He walked into the cell and set the tray on the bunk. "Eat hearty, Cullen."

The sheriff was now in the cell too, his pistol drawn. "I hear you're a real sneaky sonofabitch, Cullen."

Ben ignored the insult. "Can I see what you brung me?"

"Sure," Denton said. "But I still say it's a hell of a thing for the town to have to feed a shitass like you."

Ben leaned forward and reached out with his left hand. He grabbed the cloth and shook it. The motion caused the exact effect he was after. The two lawmen's eyes went instinctively to the movement. Ben's right hand whipped around and came out with the knife. The blade turned one quick flip before burying itself into the sheriff's belly.

He dropped his pistol and stared down at the thing sticking in him. Ben was across the room and grabbing the handle before Denton could react. The outlaw pulled the knife out and continued the motion, feeling the weapon cut deep into the deputy as he whipped it across his chest.

"Ow! You cut me!" Denton yelped.

The next attack drove the blade under the rib cage and up into vital organs. Ben twisted the knife viciously before he withdrew it.

Denton's face went white and he staggered forward, tripping over the sheriff who was now sitting down. Ben bent down to finish them off, but saw they were already dead. He walked out of the cellblock and into the office. No lanterns had been lit yet, so anyone passing outside would see nothing from any casual glances inside.

Ben went to the gunrack on the wall and selected a Winchester rifle. He found an almost-new Colt Peacemaker revolver complete with holster in a drawer full of ammunition. He stuffed his pockets with extra rounds and made sure the Winchester was fully loaded. His bundle of clothing was laying in one corner of the office. Ben picked it up and slung it over his shoulder.

A look outside informed him that darkness had descended on Red Rock. There were no street lights, only the glare from businesses and saloons that were open. He would like to have waited until it was late to make his move, but there was too much of a chance for someone to come visiting the jail.

Ben stepped quickly through the door to the boardwalk outside. He stuck to the shadows as he worked his way down the street. A couple of noisy cowboys came riding around a corner. They brandished bottles while swaying in their saddles. The two didn't go far. Their destination was the nearest saloon, and they reined up in front tying their horses to the hitching rail before staggering inside.

Ben waited a few minutes, then boldly stepped out on the boardwalk. He walked toward the horses in an easy manner, whistling softly to himself as a man might who is about to mount his own horse and ride home.

He leisurely untied one of the drunks' mounts and led it off at a slow walk. Finally he slipped his foot in the stirrup and swung up in the saddle. A group of men had gathered around a large wagon down at the edge of town. Ben pulled his hat down over his eyes and rode past them, hearing them talk among themselves. They were a bunch of farmers organizing a fence-building project.

Ben had just reached the edge of town when two riders appeared out of the gloom on the prairie. They showed strong evidence of having been on a long journey. Their horses were fatigued and trail dust was heavy on their clothing. Ben nodded politely to them as they passed.

"Howdy."

"Howdy," one replied. "Is the jail on the main street?"

Ben caught sight of the flicker of a badge under the man's vest. These would be the U.S. marshals sent out to pick him up. He had to delay them. "Nope," he lied. "You'll find it over on the south side. Ride behind them buildings there and circle around."

The lawman cursed under his breath. "You mean way over there on the far edge of town?"

"That's where it is," Ben said.

"Hell of a dumbass place to put the local lockup," the man complained.

"Thanks, mister," his pard said.

"You bet." Ben continued on, and when the time was

160

right he flicked the reins across the horse's shoulders and urged the animal into a gallop. The old thrill welled up in his emotions once more.

The run was on again.

Chapter Eleven

Ben kept the horse's gait at a fast pace for two hours after leaving Red Rock. He would have liked to maintain his speed, but gathering clouds began to obscure the moonlight. This made galloping extremely dangerous. Such things as prairie-dog holes waited for a careless rider. A running horse was sure to break a leg in one of the rodents' burrows.

They slowed to a walk, but from the animal's impatient snorting, Ben knew he really wanted to cut loose and run. He had to keep pulling in on the reins, and the outlaw knew he had made the best choice of the two available mounts when he'd gotten this one.

Ben finally decided to take a rest after dawn. He glanced around in the growing light to check for any signs of pursuit. When he was satisfied there was none, Ben rode down into a small, wooded ravine and hid himself in the trees there. He would take an hour or so of napping, then resume the trip toward the Kansas line at a cautious pace.

He hobbled the horse, and removed the saddle. He set it on the ground, arranging his other gear around it for a quick getaway if necessary. His new mount whinnied softly, and Ben patted his muzzle. "You like to run, don't you, pal?" he said fondly. "Well, you and me got the same idea of having fun, then—'cause, by God, we're gonna run from here clear up to Wichita." He pushed the animal toward an open space in the trees. "Eat some o' that sweet grass, pal. I promise I'll get you a good feed of oats up there in Kansas before I jump aboard that train for Chicago."

Ben went over to a nearby tree and sat down at its base. The time in the jail at Red Rock had been unsettling and unpleasant. The deputy's constant jibes and insults had kept Ben's nerves on edge. Between that and desperate thoughts of escape, his mind had been fully occupied. But here in this peaceful setting, alone and more relaxed, Ben's thoughts mellowed somewhat.

He remembered his room in the barn on the Baldwin farm. It would have been so nice to be able to rest there at that moment. It was dark and cool there even on a hot day. Then there was always the good, plentiful food in the kitchen. Ben had to admit to himself that those few short weeks had been among the best—if not *the* best—in his life.

He finally figured such remembrances would only make him feel worse in the end, so he leaned back and closed his eyes to do some heavy thinking before sinking into one of his usual restless cat naps.

He had a good horse and weapons with plenty of ammunition. But a search of the saddlebags showed them to be empty. The cowboy who owned the stallion evidently hadn't planned on being gone from his ranch for more than an evening in town. There was plenty of room for Ben to stuff his ammo and the bundle of clothing in them. Unfortunately there wasn't a rifle boot on the saddle, so he had to carry the Winchester with the muzzle stuck in the right-hand bag while he held onto the butt-end of the stock when he rode. It was an inconvenience he was willing to bear. The extra range of that long gun could spell the difference between escape and capture in the wide-open country where he had to travel.

Ben's big problem — aside from avoiding recapture — was food.

There was plenty of game in the area, but the last thing Ben wanted was to attract attention with gunshots — particularly if the sounds of hunting might be heard by a pursuing posse. He'd been alarmed to note the number of farms that had sprung up in the area. He could remember when a man could ride through that part of the territory for three days before he'd run into any sign of other people being around. Back in those days a fugitive could have brought a brass band along with him without alerting anyone.

The obvious answer was to steal some eats somewhere. Rustling a cow was out of the question. That would also mean making noise, then having to do some elaborate butchering. Even such an undignified thing as getting into a chicken coop could cause a racket. Ben remembered the farm hand who had worked for Jim Baldwin just before he showed up. The fellow had looted the smokehouse before leaving. That would be his own best bet too, Ben decided. Raiding a farm and getting ahold of some meat that was already butchered and ready to eat was the ticket. All that was required was to carry it away.

Ben's mind settled it all. He would wait for dark,

then scout the area as best he could until he found a smokehouse. After that, he could go hell-for-leather to the Kansas line, then turn east to Wichita.

His mind also reflected on the hopelessness of his situation under any circumstances. He had now killed three lawmen. Even if he received a presidential pardon, there would be irate starpackers who would hunt him down and kill him without mercy no matter where he might go. An outlaw would forget a pard who died in a bank or train robbery, chalking it up as part of the game. But lawmen were different. When one went down, all the others went after the killer.

Ben started to drift off to sleep. But thoughts of Arlena replaced those of his desperate planning. He had consciously concentrated on not thinking about her the way he had done about the girl Maybelle Beardsley while he was in the penitentiary. But there was a big difference between a boyhood crush and a grown man's deep love for a woman.

If he had only met her ten years earlier, he thought, then he would have gone straight and settled down. But the fact that she'd already been married at that time entered his head. Ben sighed sadly. A full and happy life was just not destined to be his. There were too many mistakes and too many regrets — except one: Ben Cullen would never regret the emotions and feelings of falling in love with Arlena.

He finally sank into a shallow sleep, waking up every five or ten minutes.

Ben divided the rest of the daylight hours between short naps and taking observation tours around the edge of the wooded area to see if any interlopers had ridden in. The countryside remained empty except for the natural prairie lushness of grass and the comings and goings of animals that lived there.

He waited until dusk before resaddling the horse and mounting up to search out a good smokehouse to rob.

The first farm he checked was a bleak, badly run outfit. The yard boasted only a crude, sod residence and an outhouse built of the same material. A tent was pitched between them, and from the look of the man, woman, and five kids who lived there, they were dirt poor. Ben wouldn't have stolen from them even if it guaranteed absolute freedom.

Ben moved on in the growing gloom. The country was so populated that he had only to travel a half hour until he reached the next farm. Although much more prosperous, there was no smokehouse visible. Perhaps the farmer there kept it as part of the barn, but Ben didn't have the time to check out that possibility.

In only twenty minutes he was at the next place. The type of structure he searched for was clearly visible. There was the house, a barn and toolshed, and an outhouse. The smokehouse was the farthest building away from the main abode. Ben smiled in satisfaction to himself. The other buildings were between the two, cutting off all view from any window if the owner happened to peer out.

There was still a bit of light, so Ben rode over to the side where the smokehouse was located. He found a handy stand of buffalo grass and concealed himself and the horse to await darkness.

There was a brief flicker of lantern light that could be seen falling outward onto the farmyard, but this was extinguished after a couple of hours. Ben waited for a bit of time to go by before he forced his horse to endure the hobble again. Then he moved down toward the farm.

His boots crunched lightly on the soil as he approached the smokehouse. When he reached the corner of the structure he stopped and listened for a couple of minutes. The only sound was the breeze playing through the barn loft, making the pulley on the haylift squeek as it swung back and forth. Ben stepped around to the door.

The dog snarled and leaped at his throat.

Ben's arm instinctively went up in front of his face. The large canine bit down hard at it, and the intruder could feel the stinging, ripping pain. The animal increased the pressure of the bite, shaking his head as if trying to drag the man down to the ground.

A door opened and a voice called out. "Shep? Shep?"

The dog couldn't bark and let go at the same time so he growled as loud as he could. But Ben's knife swiped deep across the furry throat and the dog let go.

"Shep? Heah, boy! Heah, boy!"

The blade wound was so deep that there was only a weak, gurgly growl as the hound rolled weakly on the ground, bleeding to death. Ben pulled his injured arm in close and eased the pistol from the holster with his free hand. If the man came out, there was no sense in worrying about noise.

"Shep?" There was a pause, then the man's voice was muffled a bit, showing he'd turned his head to speak inside the house. "Prob'ly scared up a coyote or fox." Then the door slammed shut.

Ben gritted his teeth against the pain, and went into the small meat-curing building. He fumbled in the dark and pulled a large hunk of meat off one of the drying racks. After stepping back outside he listened to make sure no one was coming out to investigate. Knowing that his arm was bleeding, he went back to the horse.

Ben could feel the blood seeping through his torn shirt-sleeve while he rode slowly through the night. The pain had subsided a bit, but he could not move the last two fingers of his left hand. He kept the injured limb in close and gripped the hurt part as tightly as he could to keep the bleeding under some sort of control. He rode clumsily, balancing the hunk of meat and keeping the rifle barrel under his right knee at the same time.

By the time the sun was pink on the eastern horizon, he figured he was far enough away to stop and inspect the arm. Ben gently peeled the sleeve back from the mess, and rolled it up past his elbow. The sight made him wince. Both top and bottom of the arm were badly ripped by the dog's teeth. Although no artery seemed to have been punctured, there was still plenty of bleeding.

He decided to sacrifice one of his shirts. He pulled it out of the saddlebag, and carefully cut off the sleeves with his knife. It seemed a shame to do so because of the care and cleaning that Arlena had done on the garment. But it was an absolute necessity. He wrapped them both tightly around the wound. After securing the makeshift bandages with a couple of knots, he used the rest of the shirt to wrap the meat in. He discovered, in the light, that he'd gotten ahold of a well-cured ham. He bundled it up and hung it over the saddlehorn.

Now, with the arm throbbing under the tight pressure, Ben remounted and urged the horse into a canter due north. He endured another two hours before he had to stop. His arm was throbbing badly and the makeshift dressing was completely soaked in blood. Ben got another shirt, the last one, and clumsily fashioned a sling out of it. He inserted the hurt limb inside and was somewhat relieved at the extra comfort of being able to allow it to relax. The constant strain of holding the arm to his side had caused a muscle cramp in his shoulder.

Remounting, he let his eager horse resume the pace. He found he could use the minimal guidance the animal required with pressure from his knees. He kept a northerly course as much as possible, but there were detours to be made each time a farm or small settlement popped up on the horizon.

In midafternoon, he was almost dozing off in the saddle. Between the steady, rhythmic sound of hoofbeats and the warm sun, Ben had grown sleepy. But suddenly a chill went through him. This was the old instinct developed over the years of being chased.

He stood up in the stirrups and looked back.

There were two of them. Both riders had spread out so they could approach from separate wide-spread angles. Ben put the reins in the hand of his hurt arm and grasped the Winchester with the other.

"Ha-*yahh*!" he yelled and kicked the horse's flanks. The animal leaped forward and broke into a gallop in a joyous burst of energy.

The first shot zapped across Ben's nose. He jerked his bad arm from the sling. "Damn!" he said aloud in pain, but he was happy to see he could use the rifle. He squeezed off a round in the direction of the nearest man, then swung over and cut loose on the other.

The chase got serious then. Ben forgot about shooting. It was useless anyhow, since accuracy was completely out of the question. Ben put all his effort on the escape. The run streaked across open, flat areas and down into gentle gulleys.

Occasional shots ricocheted by, zinging off into the wide expanse of open space. Although the noise was impressive, these were not close. It would take a wildly lucky shot for one man on a galloping horse to shoot another man speeding along the same way.

Ben dipped into another gulley and pounded across a shallow creek, sending muddy splashes of water flying. He climbed the other side and urged his mount to greater speed. Ben's plan was not to continue running. That would have eventually led him into a spot where he'd be pinned in or cut off. A farm or town might crop up at any time. And there was also the possibility that the two gunmen chasing him had pals out in the area somewhere too.

What Ben needed was a place to hole up and shoot it out. But there was no place to be found. The terrain had turned flat again and there wasn't as much as a single tree around to use as cover. The situation had to be brought under control and damned near immediately.

Ben pulled on the reins, and turned around.

He charged straight back toward the startled pursuers. They continued to press on, shooting at him now, and with the range rapidly decreasing there was a damned good chance they'd knock him out in the saddle. Ben let the reins go and held the Winchester in his bad hand. He drew the revolver with the other and leaned low over the horse's neck.

Once again he chose the nearest man for his target. Ben stuck the pistol out and fired three times. The second round caught the man in the abdomen. He suddenly bent over in the saddle and rode past. Ben wheeled around again in time to see the gunman slip from the saddle and hit the ground hard, rolling over several times before stopping and lying still.

His partner, full of spit and fight, had also turned around. Ben galloped toward him. He waited until they were close together. Both passed each other firing ineffective shots.

The two adversaries raced in a circle, keeping up a steady rate of fire. Now Ben's pistol was empty but he still had fourteen rounds left in the Winchester rifle. He cut loose with three of these as their circling grew tighter and tighter.

Then Ben made his move.

He reined in sharply and leaped down from the saddle. Standing up he took a quick bead on his adversary and pulled the trigger.

The .44 caliber round hit its target solidly. The man looked like he'd leaped sideways out of the saddle. He hit the ground kicking up a cloud of dust. Ben, cranking in another bullet, walked toward him. There was no movement from the gunman except for a slow flexing of one leg. Then he was still. Ben, still cautious, slowly approached until he stood over him.

The wound was ghastly. The big slug had splintered, blowing out a large portion of the right side. Ben could see his innards, red and green, in the bloody mess. The dead man's eyes were wide open and full of dirt.

Ben turned and walked back to the horse. Mounting, he rode toward the other fallen pursuer. The fellow was sitting up. He attempted to hold up his hands to show he would offer no resistance. But the effort caused him to topple over. Ben also came up slowly on this one.

No doubt the lawman was alive. That meant he was still a potential and dangerous threat.

Ben swung out of the saddle. "Don't move them hands."

"Lemme sit up," the man said weakly. "It hurts to lean over."

"You gutshot?" Ben asked.

"Yeah."

"Okay. But if you as much as frown, I'm gonna put the next one through your head."

"You'd prob'ly do me a favor if you did." The man, wearing a badge, struggled to straighten up. "I ain't got no fight left," he said with a hint of pleading in his voice.

Ben picked up the man's carbine and tossed it away. "I ain't gonna shoot you no more."

The lawman believed him. "Obliged."

Ben studied his face. "Didn't I see you in Red Rock?"

"Yeah. Me an' Hammond seen you when we rode in." He forced a grin. "You give us the wrong direction to the jailhouse."

"You two U.S. marshals?"

"Yeah. Outta Guthrie. I'm Tom Price."

"Howdy. I reckon you know my name."

"Sure do, Cullen," Price said.

"How many o' you jaspers come after me?" Ben asked.

"Just the two of us. We found the sheriff and deputy you cut up," Price said. "The deputy's dead but the sheriff's fine."

"I thought he was dead too," Ben said.

Price shook his head. "Nope. Getting cut like that just scared the shit out of him. The town doc even says he wasn't too serious."

"I don't think you are either," Ben said. "You might just make it. But your pard is dead."

"You sure?"

"His whole side was blowed out," Ben said.

Price nodded his head. "He was the one who tracked you. He was madder'n hell when we finally figgered out it was you we seen when we come into town. He finally wanted a hunk o' your ass, Cullen."

"Turned out the other way around, though," Ben said.

Price pointed to Ben's arm. "What happened?"

"Just a damn dawg bite," Ben said. "Nothing serious."

"You're bleeding," Price said. "It's running down your fingers."

"You're bleeding, too," Ben said. He looked at Price for several more moments, then glanced out and saw Price's horse calmly grazing some fifty yards distance. He slowly walked across the grass to the animal. The horse calmly watched him approach, then allowed itself to be led back. Ben held onto the reins. "I ain't gonna help you into the saddle, Price. But I'll put down whatever you need outta your gear for you."

"Just gimme the bags and my blankets," Price said.

"I can't have you riding back to some farmhouse and spreading the word," Ben said.

"Yeah," Price said in understanding.

"Somebody might be by," Ben said.

"Ain't likely."

"Nope. But if it's any comfort, I'll tell 'em about you if they catch me," Ben said.

"Obliged."

The fugitive searched the saddlebags to make sure there were no weapons hidden in them. All he found was whiskey, bandages, beef jerky, and dried beans. He also pulled off the lawman's canteen. "I'll leave this too and go get your pard's. Dying o' thirst can be worse'n a gunshot."

"Maybe I'll die of a combination of both," Price said.

"Save the whiskey for last," Ben advised him. "Sometimes it's better to cash in your chips drunk than sober."

"Can I have Hammond's whiskey too?"

"He's got likker with him?"

"Yep."

But Ben shook his head. "I need that whiskey for my arm. But you'll get his saddlebags too."

Price took a deep breath and grimaced as a wave of pain went through him. "Y'know, Cullen, if somebody comes by I just might make it."

"You might."

Ben forked his saddle and rode back to where the dead man lay in the undignified position with his entrails out in the grass. There were already big blowflies buzzing around the body. Ben got his horse and led him back to Price. Once more he dumped some supplies at the man's feet. "I'm gonna take his guns and bullets," he said, putting a pair of Remington .44s in his own saddlebags.

"If they catch you, Cullen, I'll tell 'em how you done me right," Price promised.

"Shit! You'll be dead in four or five days, Price," Ben said. He got back up in his saddle. "But I reckon you can be glad the Injuns ain't around no more."

"I surely am," Price said.

"So long."

"Obliged."

Ben again turned north and resumed the run.

The dead marshal's whiskey wasn't drunk by Ben Cullen. Instead, he kept his bloody bandages soaked in the stuff. There were two bottles, but from the amount he used on the dog bite they would only last a couple of days. He wished he'd kept Price's, but somehow he couldn't gutshoot a man and take his liquor too.

His hand outside the bandage was now badly swollen. It had turned purple, and the discoloration was creeping slowly down toward the two fingers that remained without feeling. No matter how hard he tried, he couldn't move them. They were numb, as if they had died on their own.

It wasn't so bad in the cooler morning or evening, but the wound bothered him terribly during the hot afternoon while the sun blazed down on the prairie. Waves of nausea swept over Ben, and he had to dismount a couple of times to vomit.

Finally, the afternoon after the gunfight, his vision blurred and reddened. Ben felt himself swaying in the saddle and he dismounted. He hung on to the saddlehorn as dizziness swept over him in pulsating waves. He felt his grip weaken and his knees buckled.

The next thing he knew he was lying down. He rolled over on his hands and knees to vomit again.

There was an awful thirst in his throat and he staggered back to the saddle to get his canteen. Tipping it up, he drained the metal container in greedy, loud gulps.

Again he hung on to that saddlehorn until he felt better. It was a hell of an effort but he got himself into the saddle. The horse, sensing its rider's weakness, went slowly, but Ben again slipped from the saddle. Finally, as he groped back to his feet, he admitted to himself what he had been pushing back farther and farther from conscious thought:

The dog bite had turned into a serious wound.

Chapter Twelve

After Ben Cullen left his pal Elmer Woods on the doctor's porch in Fort Smith, Arkansas, he had only a short distance to go before he was in an area that could have rightly been described as Outlaw Heaven.

This land, the Indian Territory, was located just across the Arkansas River from Fort Smith. It was a wild region peopled by the five civilized tribes — the Cherokees, Choctaws, Creeks, Seminoles, and Chickasaws — a few decent whites, and bands of outlaws using the unhappy place as a haven from the law. These brigands left their hideouts only to pillage and kill in the settled areas. They also did a lot of the same in the Territory, where only a handful of Indian police was detailed to keep the peace.

The situation was made doubly bad by the fact that these native lawmen had no jurisdiction over the white outlaws, only their own brethren. The whites could only be arrested and brought to justice by marshals out of Judge Isaac Parker's Federal court in Fort Smith Arkansas. The vastness of the job, and the few men to administer justice there, created a violent environment that suited the lawbreakers fine.

Ben Cullen's introduction to the Indian Territory began with a brief, violent encounter that marked the first time he killed a man. Despite the numerous bank and train robberies he had participated in as a member of the Gilray gang, Ben had yet to shoot down another human being. True, he fired plenty of bullets, but he took no pleasure in the thought of gunning down another man. Besides, he wasn't much of a shot, and he did the wild, quick shooting mostly just to make other folks slow down or duck their heads while he and his pards made their galloping bids for escape.

Ben had ridden hard after leaving Fort Smith and didn't really feel safe until he'd arrived in Muskogee. He could tell from the look of the place as he rode in that no warrant-serving marshal would be waiting for him, and there was even less chance that one might happen to show up. Legal authority made only occasional appearances in Muskogee. The town was a wide-open, wild place where each man made his own law and backed it up with carbine and pistol.

Since leaving prison and joining Gilray's bunch Ben had developed a fondness for bourbon whiskey. He wasn't a drunk by any stretch of the imagination, but he had learned to enjoy getting mellow and intoxicated with some good sipping bourbon that he took slowly and without much talking. He did this privately, wrapped up in his own thoughts. After the hell of a botched train robbery and leaving off a badly-shot-up pal, the one thing that Ben Cullen needed by the time he hit Muskogee was a few good stiff drinks.

He rode down the main street and spotted a saloon that looked a bit better than the rest. He wasn't fastidious about where he imbibed, Ben just figured the fancier the saloon the better the chance for less-watered-down bourbon.

After tying off his horse at the rail, Ben went inside and bellied up to the bar. The establishment wasn't luxurious by any standards—except Muskogee's. It was a frame building so hastily erected that there were open places where the planking had warped. The floor was hardpacked dirt covered with sawdust to soak up the spit and the blood. The bar itself was only two-by-sixes laid across a line of barrels, and the man who worked behind it wasn't a talkative type. When Ben approached, the barkeep just raised an inquiring eyebrow.

"Bourbon," Ben said. "A bottle."

The man set the whiskey down and plunked a reasonably clean glass beside it. "Four bits."

Ben paid and poured himself a drink. He took it, as he did all the first ones, fast. He threw it back in his throat and let it burn itself down, clearing out the trail dust. He served himself another. This time he took just a sip, held it in his mouth to enjoy the flavor, and swallowed.

The whiskey loosened him up some and made the world seem not such a bad place. He continued his slow drinking. Now and then he would glance around. This was more out of habit than of real curiosity about the other bar patrons. Ben was in no mood for company. An old habit from Leavenworth kept him from looking directly into any one man's eyes. In prison this could be an invitation to various kinds of trouble. But each time his gaze roved, he noted one black-jowled man who was looking directly at him. This penitentiary etiquette worked both ways too. The man was clearly giving his undivided attention to Ben, and it started to rile him. Finally, he responded.

"Is there something you want?" Ben asked.

The man's eyes continued to bore into his own. "You drink hard for a little feller."

Ben knew he had a troublemaker on his hands. This was a fellow whose bad temper got worse with a bellyful of liquor, and like most barroom brawlers, he looked for trouble from men he figured would be easy to whip. As a small man Ben was used to larger bullies trying to pick on him. It would have been best to leave, but there was another convict habit he couldn't break — a man's reputation either made him or broke him. Backing down could be as bad as suicide. He had to respond. "You worried about the likker supply here?" Ben asked.

"Not much," the man allowed. "If'n I run short I'll take yours."

The barkeep's taciturn demeanor changed. "If you two jaspers want trouble, take it outside."

Ben defended himself. "I'm minding my own business and you can see that."

"Get on outside," the barkeep said. "I don't need your trouble here."

Ben's face reddened with fury. "The hell if I will." He pointed to his adversary. "If he'd mind his own business

180

there wouldn't be no trouble. Anyhow, are you afraid o' that feller? Is that why you're telling me to leave instead o' him?"

The large man laughed. "I'll take care of getting you outside, Shorty." He stepped away from the bar.

Ben knew he could never have whipped the man. "I don't like working up a sweat. You come near me and you die." The challenge was loud and clear. He pulled his pistol and stood ready.

There was a crash of chairs and scuffle of feet across the floor as everyone in the room—including the barkeep—made plenty of room.

"Shit," the bully said. "Can't you take some funning? You don't have to throw down on a feller." He looked to the others in the saloon for support. "It's a hell of a thing to pull a shooting iron over a damned joke."

But the small crowd wasn't impressed with him. There were even a few disapproving remarks. Most of these had to do with someone starting trouble, then not having the sand to finish it.

"I'm telling you loud and clear," Ben said. "Leave me be or I'll plug you."

"Relax, Shorty," the other sneered. He tried to make himself look better by facing Ben for an extra few moments. Finally he turned and walked toward the rear of the saloon.

Ben sat his pistol where it would be handy on the bar, and went back to his bottle.

The shot inside the closed-in space of the barroom was so loud that it made Ben's ears ring. The two that quickly followed didn't seem quite so loud to his numbed eardrums. But the chunks of wood flying out of the bar were plenty unnerving without the thundering noise.

Ben didn't remember grabbing his pistol, but he did so with a speed born out of the startled fear. He returned fire, squeezing the trigger three times while aiming hastily and in panic. Two more shots came from the bully before Ben fired again, but the effect of that final shot was impressive.

The man's front teeth shattered and his jaw blew off to one side. He staggered backward and Ben fired his final bullet. It punched dead center and knocked the bully flat on his back. Ben quickly reloaded in the moment of silence that followed.

"Fair fight," somebody finally said.

"Yeah," another echoed. "Fair fight."

"I'll take the bottle with me," Ben said.

"Yes, sir," the barkeep responded.

Ben kept low the next couple of days in case the man had any friends, but it became obvious the bully was either a loner or just plain ornery enough to be unpopular. After Ben returned to the saloon for another bottle, he found everyone a bit friendlier and he fell in with a group of men who invited him along on a cattle-rustling run south into Texas.

This opened new vistas for Ben Cullen, and he spent the next three years roaming with various groups of pardners. They hit ranches not only in Texas and the Indian Territory, but even went as far as old Mexico.

And there he killed his second man.

This was a *vaquero* off a ranch that Ben and the bunch he was running with at that time had raided. It was a chance shot while being pursued, but there was no denying it had been his bullet that spilled the Mexican from the saddle. The situation was one of bellowing men, discharging pistols and rifles, and the combined thunder of both horse and cattle hooves on the gravelly ground. Mexican cowboys were fearless even when they weren't angry. Once enraged they were *tigres bravos*. A hell of a running gunbattle developed out of the incident.

Ben fired backward, sometimes without even looking, emptying one pistol and bringing out the other before he managed to hit the fierce pursuer who dogged his tracks.

When the stolen cattle were taken to Paco's for disposal, his pards had boasted of his shooting skill, and Ben got an undeserved reputation for being fast and accurate. The fact was that Ben just didn't have the eye and hand coordination necessary to be a dead-shot. But he had cool enough nerves to stand in the line of fire and patiently trade bullets with an adversary until one of them fell. What Ben Cullen really had was plenty of luck.

He continued to move around that part of the country until he was not only running into marshals from Judge Parker's court, but also getting into conflicts with those out of the brand-new U.S. marshal's office in Guthrie after the Cherokee Strip was established. Some of the lawmen assigned from that jurisdiction were old adversaries like Chris Madsen and Heck Thomas. And he ran into a new one by the name of United States Deputy Marshal Jack Macon.

When Ben Cullen and Jack Macon met, the marshal was tied to a chair on T. C. Hutchins's ranch south of the town of Perry. Hutchins had a few miserable cattle and paid a half dozen hard-bitten cowboys to keep an eye on them, but his real money was made in conjunction with Paco Chavez when he mingled stolen cattle in with his own, to make minor drives up to the railroad at Perry to ship them to market. If any of the townspeople had bothered to take notice or count the amount of cattle going through the Hutchins' spread, they would have figured something was fishy.

But in Oklahoma Territory a man minded his own business unless there was a threat to his life or property.

Jack Macon was a stubborn, dedicated lawman. He had known there was somebody disposing of stolen herds for rustlers, but he could never quite figure out who it was. Finally, piecing together a combination of evidence, rumor, and official reports, he narrowed the culprit down to somewhere in the Perry area. He got permission from Chief Marshal E. D. Nix to make a lone investigation into the matter. When Macon got to Perry, he began a patient task of scouting, checking out each ranch in the region until, to his bad luck, he came to Hutchins's place.

T. C. Hutchins, being a naturally nervous man, kept a strict system of sentries and patrols. His boys roamed the property regularly, doing so carefully to catch any snoopers or lawmen that may have gotten wise to the setup. That was how Jack Macon got caught.

The deputy marshal was lying on the crest of a ravine peering at the ranch house when three of Hutchins's men discovered him. Normally they would have shot him on the spot, but when they noted who he was they decided to settle a couple of old scores at their leisure with one or two Comanche tricks they knew about.

Ben Cullen and three of Paco's men arrived that same evening with a small herd to ship north. Ben was the ramrod of the outfit, and he went in the house to pass on Paco's instructions for the proper disposal of the cattle.

T. C. Hutchins introduced the two men. He wasn't particularly affable about it. "Ben Cullen," he said. "I'd like you to meet Jack Macon. He's the dumbest sonofabitch in Oklahoma Territory."

Ben looked down at the bound man. "Howdy." Then he glanced at T. C. "Any particular reason you got him tied to that chair?"

"Yep," T. C. said. "The boys is gonna roast him." He laughed. "That there's a United States deputy marshal out of Nix's office in Guthrie."

"Yeah? What's his name again?"

"My name," Macon interrupted, "is Jack Macon and you better remember it, 'cause I'll remember yours, Ben Cullen. And I promise I'll see all you sonofabitches in the territorial penitentiary!"

Ben admired his courage, but couldn't recommend the man's good sense. "Any particular reason I should let a feller roped down like you order me in to prison?"

"Don't worry none," Macon said. "I'll be taking you in."

"I admire grit in a man," Ben said. "I truly do." He laughed and sat down at a nearby table to do his business with Hutchins. When they were finished, Ben stopped to say good bye to the lawman before leaving. "Any particular time you want me to show up at the territorial prison?"

Macon snarled. "I'll get you there myself when the time is right, you sawed-off little bastard!"

Ben only smiled. "So long," He decided to egg the man on a bit. "Just in case I forget, what's your name again?"

"Macon, damn your eyes! Jack Macon, U.S. deputy marshal."

"Well, don't forget me neither. I'm Cullen, damn *your* eyes! Ben Cullen, U.S. cattle rustler."

Hutchins almost fell over laughing, but something in Macon's gaze cause an involuntary twinge of uneasiness in Ben. He displayed an uneasy grin, then took his leave.

Ben went back to cattle rustling for a few months, plus a train robbery in the Cherokee Strip, before he returned to the Hutchins' spread. He'd forgotten about the feisty marshal in the meantime, but being back in the ranch house reminded him of the lawman.

"Say," he asked T. C. Hutchins over a cup of hot coffee. "What'd you fellers do to that starpacker you had tied to the chair?"

"You see the chair is gone," Hutchins said.

Ben looked around. "I reckon."

"Well, the ornery sonofabitch busted it up and got outta here. No guns and no boots, but he stole a damn mule outta my corral and lit out for Guthrie," Hutchins said.

Ben laughed out loud.

"It ain't funny!" Hutchins snapped. "He killed Lanky

Duval with the leg o' that godamned chair. Flat beat him to death with it!" The rancher-rustler calmed down, but pointed a finger into Ben's face and spoke low. "That Macon knows you, Ben Cullen."

"Shit!" Ben scoffed. "He won't remember me. He didn't see me 'cept for a few minutes."

"That's be long enough for Macon," Hutchins said. "But you was here for a coupla hours, Ben. Not a few minutes."

Ben only laughed again. "Cut out the shit, Hutch. Let's do some whiskey drinking. It's a long way back to Paco's tomorrow."

But Marshal Jack Macon did remember Ben, and it was only a matter of a few months their trails crossed again.

This time it was an ambush just south of the Texas line. Ben and some of his erstwhile cronies had hit none other than the U.S. Army at Fort Sill. A new shipment of recently purchased government horses, still to have the "U.S." brand put on their flanks, was corraled at an outlying area of the post. The outlaws swept down on them, killing one soldier and wounding three others, then broke the small herd loose and headed them south toward a Mexican market.

Jack Macon, active as usual, had intelligence on the horse buyers south of the border. He and some five other deputies had been patrolling along the Red River. They had been using a small cavalry encampment as a headquarters, and the news of the daring theft reached there via military telegraph.

Macon had a good idea of the thieves' destination, and he headed toward a spot where there would be a good chance to ambush them.

This was a narrow cut in the bluffs on the Texas side. Here, concealed in the heights, they would have any passersby caught between them a deep, rapid-running portion of the river.

Macon like to kill people, and he waited impatiently for more than thirty hours before the objects of his attention finally arrived. Although the marshal's force was small, the outlaws were hemmed in tight. The first salvo of carbine and rifle fire immediately knocked three of the seven outlaws out of their saddles.

The horses stampeded and took off leaving the four survivors — including Ben Cullen — exposed. They wheeled helplessly around on their own mounts as more lead was poured into their midst. Two more went down, leaving Ben and a wild-eyed kid from New Mexico riding back and forth.

Macon and his pals played games with the two. The outlaws were allowed to ride freely until they reached a point close the the end of the bluffs. Then the firing built up, forcing them back to the center. Even the kill-crazy Macon wanted a prisoner or two out of the situation, so he ordered his men to cease fire when their quarry once again was driven inward.

There was only a fifty-yard distance down to the river from the cliffs, and the U.S. marshal had recognized one of the horse thieves. He took a deep breath and shouted, "How're you doing down there, Ben Cullen?"

Ben, unable to spot anyone on the bluffs, kept his rifle held ready. "I'm having a nice afternoon. Who's that?"

"Macon—Jack Macon—you little peckerhead," he yelled back. "You and your pard throw down them guns and we'll take you in to Guthrie. How's that?"

Ben licked his lips. He didn't figure he'd be hanged, since the law couldn't prove he actually shot any of the soldiers back at Fort Sill. But there was at least a thirty-year stretch in the Oklahoma Territorial Prison waiting for him. He looked over at his pard. "What do you say?"

"I'm going into the river."

"You'll never make it," Ben warned him.

The other rustler only grinned, then suddenly wheeled his horse and sped toward the water. Neither he nor the animal got beyond ten yards before the volleys did them in.

A split second after the kid had made his move, Ben slipped down on the other side of his own horse on the far side from the lawmen as he took his chance. He got a good couple of seconds to get up some speed, but that was enough. Before the lawmen could draw a bead on him, he had streaked out of the dangerous area and pounded over the prairie toward freedom.

Ben evaded escape for three days before he was sure he'd made it to freedom for certain.

The affair enraged Macon and he made it his own personal crusade to bring Ben Cullen to justice—either in handcuffs or laid across the back of a horse.

Ben made contact with the marshal off and on for the next four years. Finally, Macon had gotten so close that Ben decided to change his lifestyle. The close calls and explosive gunfights taught him a lot of respect for Jack Macon's tenacity. Ben took a breather for a while and stopped riding the owlhoot trail. He decided to lay low by seeking anonymity in the guise of a hand on some secluded ranch. The Texas panhandle offered the best opportunities with its seemingly limitless expanses and wide separation of cattle outfits. Ben finally found a small place and hired on.

That situation had come to a conclusion on a dark, moonless August night of the year 1901.

Chapter Thirteen

A sharp jolt of pain brought Ben Cullen out of his deep, troubled sleep. He sat up knowing too well that he had rolled over on his dog-bitten arm. Ben gently held and caressed the injured limb.

Suddenly he noticed that the sun was mid-morning high. The realization brought a stab of panic—as shocking as the hurt in his arm—but it quickly subsided as he checked out the campsite he had established the previous evening. All was serene, and the only sounds were those of birds, insects, and the gentle wafting of the water stroking past the bank.

He had slept through the entire night, but rather than enjoying the deep, dreamless rest experienced on the Baldwin farm, the previous night's slumber had been full of disjointed, disturbing dreams. The fever had caused his memories to travel across his mind in wavery, uneven images that went as far back as his boyhood in Pleasanton. During one episode, he had been standing at the fence of the Beardsley's home. Oren Beardsley had called in a posse to chase him away. The horsemen, shooting wildly, chased him across a dreamscape of ravines and creeks while Maybelle Beardsley ran alongside him shouting taunts and insults. That nightmare evolved into another in which he was back in Leavenworth Penitentiary. This time he was unarmed while Marshal Jack Macon chased him up and down the cell tiers firing at him until Ben left the blockhouse and raced for the safety of the mineshaft. But Morley Jackson and his gang of prison rapists were waiting for him there—armed and mounted. They chased Ben back toward Macon. And Maybelle Beardsley was there too, standing by the railing of a guardtower, pointing and laughing at him. Suddenly it turned night and the prison yard was drenched in the pale yellow glare of the watch lanterns. A movement in the door of the infirmary caught his eye, and Ben saw Arlena standing in the doorway of the prison hospital. Her dress was unbuttoned and her breasts were exposed to him in the moonlight. Morley Jackson spotted the woman and let out a bellow of lustful delight. He turned toward her. Ben wanted to save the woman he loved, but now he could hardly move as he tried to run toward the door where she stood.

It was at that point that he'd tossed and turned until he rolled over on the arm and woke up.

Despite these horrible dreams, the sleep had done Ben some good. He felt fairly rested, though his wound still hurt like hell. The faithful horse, hobbled nearby, languidly nibbled on the sweet prairie grass near the bank of the river. A grove of cottonwoods shielded the camp from sight and offered a windbreak at the same time.

Ben got to his feet and was somewhat relieved to note that the usual dizziness was not so strong. It was obvious he would have to travel slow and rest plenty if he was to continue his journey, however. Ben took his time saddling the horse and gathering up his gear. His left hand was almost useless, but he could still manage without much trouble. He was just starting to slip his foot in the stirrup when the sound of someone walking toward him sounded in the cottonwoods around the camp.

Ben drew his pistol while his eyes darted about, picking the best route out of the brush. The noise continued until two boys suddenly crashed into the open area. The pair, with fishing poles over their shoulders, stopped when they saw Ben.

"Howdy, mister," one said.

Ben nodded. "How're you boys doing?" He stood on the far side of the horse, and they couldn't see he'd drawn the six-shooter.

"Perty good," the more gabby one answered. "You're right here at our best fishing spot."

Ben glanced back toward the river. "Well, now, that looks like the right place, all right."

The second boy, smaller and less talkative, was eager to fish. He went directly over to the bank and began preparing his line. His pal was more inclined to conversation. "Did you do any fishing here, mister?"

"Nope," Ben answered. "Didn't have the time." By then he'd figured out the boys were alone, so he reholstered the revolver. "I got to get to Kansas."

"You're in Kansas, mister," the boy said. "If you're

193

headed toward Liberal, it's another ten miles west." The boy squinted his eyes as he looked closer at Ben. "Or are you with the posse?"

"Posse?"

"Them fellers from the Territory," the boy said. "Say, did you ever find the outlaw you're hunting?"

"Not that I know of," Ben said. He held up his arm. "My horse throwed me and I hurt my arm, so I let the others go on ahead." He paused to note the kid was buying his story. "So I'd better go on and find 'em. Do you know which direction they went?"

"Yes, sir. They was going to Liberal," the boy said. "I heard 'em when they talked with my pa at our farm. They was pretty well scattered around, but ever'one was to meet there in town and either hunt some more for the bad man or go back home."

"I'll meet up with 'em there," Ben said.

"They say that outlaw is a mean'un," the boy said. "According to one o' them Oklahoma fellers, he's a cold-blooded killer with the look o' the devil in his eye."

"That's right, boy," Ben said. "I swear he's eight foot tall and you know what else . . . " He let the question hang for effect.

"What?" the boy asked eagerly.

"He's got a tail," Ben said.

The boy scoffed. "Aw!"

"He sure does!" Ben said. "And that jasper keeps the thing coiled up and tied to his back."

"Lord above!"

Ben swung up into the saddle. "Well, son, I don't want to run into that big feller with the tail while I'm alone, so's I reckon I better get over to Liberal and find my pards. That's ten miles west, huh?"

"Yes, sir."

"Obliged, boy. I hope the fishing's good. So long."

"So long, mister." The kid, suddenly remembering why he'd gone there in the first place, wasted no time in rushing toward his friend down on the river bank. Ben could hear him shouting to his little friend, "Hey, Tommy Joe! Did you hear about that outlaw?"

Ben, grinning despite his physical discomfort, rode out of the trees and went due north until he was well beyond the campsite. When he was sure that neither one of the boys could see him, he turned east.

The ground rolled in swells in that part of Kansas and the grass was thick and high. Although there were not many trees, that sort of terrain offered cover in the form of depressions and ravines. Once, hundreds of thousands of buffalo had thrived on the lush prairie land, but they and the noble Plains Indians who hunted them were gone. Now farms and towns were spotted across the mighty expanse of earth, and barbed wire was making its insidious inroad on a land where both men and animals had once known complete freedom.

Ben had to continue his zigzag journey to avoid these places of habitat. Between that and his slow pace, he made very little progress in miles traveled. Once more he weakened in the pounding heat of the afternoon sun, and the throbbing began in his arm, sending streaks of pain up as high as his shoulder. When he took the time to cut off a hunk of the ham to eat, he thought of the terrible price he'd paid for the meat.

The situation grew worse as the afternoon's ride

continued. Waves of nausea and faintness swept over him. A few times, Ben was forced to slip out of the saddle and hang on until the sickness passed. Each time the horse, sensing its rider's distress, stood patiently still until Ben laboriously pulled himself back up to continue the ride.

The bandage seemed to grow tighter around the arm, but Ben knew this was because the swelling was increasing. The fingers were now thick and purple, swollen so badly that the fingernails looked like they'd been pushed down into the swollen flesh. Fortunately, there were plenty of creeks in the area. Ben stopped and stuck the arm in the cooling water each time he crossed one. This would bring the swelling down a bit, but within a quarter of an hour the good effects of the soaking would wear off.

Finally Ben felt so worn and exhausted that he needed to stop until the next day. He'd spotted a line of trees a mile away that gave promise not only to a good hiding place, but to the water he would need to nurse himself. He swung the horse in that direction and rode slowly to the spot.

He found a narrow, shallow creek there. The rapidly flowing water was noisy as it rolled over the rocky bed that was bounded by grass and clover. Ben dismounted and tended the horse first. Then he lay down his blankets and arranged them so he could use the saddle as a pillow. Then he settled down and gently laid his arm across his stomach. Within minutes he'd fallen into another one of the disturbing naps that took him from deep slumber to restless sleep in alternating, feverish waves.

"Wake up, mister!"

Ben's eyes came open and he saw the two men looking down at him. Each had a carbine pointed dead on his chest. He licked his lips as the sleepiness evaporated and the fear took over. "Yeah?"

"You just stay the way you are," the larger, darker one said. "I think you're just the feller we're looking for."

The other left them to rifle through Ben's saddlebags. "There ain't nothing in here but bullets and some clothes, Bob."

The man called Bob didn't take his eyes off Ben. "Is there any red checkedy shirts in there? The sheriff said he had one like that in the bundle."

"Nope."

"Just a minute, Jim," Bob said. He nudged Ben with his boot. "What's the matter with your arm?"

"My horse throwed me," Ben said. "Can I sit up? I feel silly laying down here."

"Go ahead," Bob said. "But don't try nothing. What's your name?"

"Fred Jones," Ben said.

"You sure it ain't Ben Cullen?" Jim said, coming back over.

"I oughta know my own name," Ben said.

"To hell with your name," Bob said. He looked closer at the bandage on Ben's arm. "That used to be a red checkedy shirt. I can see that even through the blood on it."

Ben noticed that the man named Jim was a cross-draw type. The butt of the holstered revolver stuck out conveniently into Ben's face. That was his favorite kind

197

to be captured by. "How come you fellers is bothering me?"

"We're part of a posse outta Red Rock in the territory," Jim said. "And if you're Ben Cullen, you killed our deputy and stuck a knife in the sheriff. You—" He stopped. "Looky at that saddle! I swear that's the one that was on Crease's horse that was stolen." He glared at the fugitive. "You rustled that horse in Red Rock, didn't you?"

"Hell, no!" Ben protested. "I didn't steal nothing nowhere. You fellers got no right to talk to me like this."

Jim motioned at Ben. "Move over, godammit!"

Ben got to his knees and moved to his left. Jim walked up to check the saddle, and Ben's hand shot out at the cross-draw holster. He pulled the pistol loose and fired in almost the same motion. Jim jumped straight up in the air and fell down in a heap.

"You little bastard!" Bob bellowed. He fired a quick shot from the carbine that zapped past Ben's face.

Ben swung the pistol revolver toward him, pulling the trigger. He missed while Bob worked the cocking lever to chamber another round. Ben shot again and missed. Bob brought the carbine up while Ben fired twice in panicky jerks of the trigger.

Both rounds hit the man and he stumbled backward with a puzzled, angry expression on his face. He died without closing his eyes.

Ben couldn't waste time resaddling his own horse. The sounds of the shots might have alerted other members of the posse. There was every possibility he would be in for a wild, shooting ride. After grabbing his own saddlebags and Winchester rifle, he mounted Bob's horse and crashed blindly through the trees to the open prairie.

The run continued.

Chapter Fourteen

On the afternoon of the day following the shooting of the two possemen, Ben Cullen's arm was hurting so bad it forced him to make a dramatic and dangerous decision.

He would seek out a doctor.

Although such an action would surely set the law straight on him, there was no choice. If a physician helped him, Ben would never be able to bring himself to silence him with a bullet. Because of this aversion to cold-blooded murder, the best chance he had — and it was a slim one — was to remain as anonymous as possible with the hope that the doctor would not inform any lawmen of his presence.

The arm was festering badly, and his own physical condition was deteriorating so fast that he couldn't even monitor it himself. Ben consoled himself with the wild hope that all a doctor would have to do would be to lance, clean, and rebandage the wound. Once that was done, with any luck, recovery would only be a matter of time.

Ben's arrival at the town of Medicine Lodge was timely. It was just past dusk and there were few people about. Ben rode slowly onto the nearly deserted main street to search out any sign of a local doctor. His feverish red eyes burned as he scanned the handpainted signs mounted over the storefronts. Although he could barely read, he knew he would recognize the words he sought if he saw them.

"Hey, mister. Who're you looking for?"

Ben, startled, had failed to notice the man in the shadows on the boardwalk. "What?" he said awkwardly.

The man stepped out where he was easier to see. He was a cheerful-looking portly citizen, wearing a cocky derby. "I seen you riding down the street. Even a fool like me could see you was looking for something."

"I need a doctor," Ben said. "My horse throwed me."

"I'll say you do! That hand looks badly swole up." The stranger pointed down on the street. "He's just on the other side o' Woods's general store there. Fact o' the matter, he rented the space from Elmer."

"Elmer? Elmer Woods?" Ben asked.

"Sure. You know him?"

"Naw, I guess not," Ben lied. Memories of Elmer Woods in the Gilray gang flooded Ben's tortured mind. The last time he'd seen his old friend had been a similar situation. But it was Elmer who'd been left bleeding on a physician's front porch in Fort Smith, Arkansas.

"Obliged," Ben said.

"Sure," the man said. "The doc lives there. You can wake him up."

Ben rode down the street to the general store. He

had a completely different idea in mind now. He looked at the store, then let the horse carry him around the corner to the alley. He came back up behind the business and stopped. Ben dismounted and tied the horse to the back of a shed directly in back of the store. When he was sure the animal was secure and out of sight, he went to the door. It took him only a few moments to work the hasp loose. He let himself in and stumbled around in the dark until he found a comfortable place on some feedsacks.

Ben drew his pistol and settled down. He drifted into a restless slumber, hoping like hell that this was the Elmer Woods he'd ridden with on the owlhoot trail such a long, long time before.

Thin, red shafts of the rising sun shot through the windowpanes of the back room. Ben had hardly slept because of pain the previous night. He shifted his position on the feedsacks and groaned softly.

There was a loud click from the front of the store.

Ben eased himself to his feet and walked quietly to the back door to peer out into the establishment. In the light he could see a profitable-looking operation with plenty of merchandise arranged neatly on shelves. A long counter ran the length of the building. Ben's eyes jerked toward the door as it opened.

Elmer Woods looked pretty much the same. He was heavier, a lot thinner on top, and sported a paunch that showed his life was a most comfortable one.

Ben made sure his old friend was alone, then stepped out of the back room. "Elmer."

Elmer almost jumped. "Who the hell—"

"It's me. Ben Cullen."

Elmer hurried toward the back. "Goddamn, Ben! It is you!"

Ben forced a grin. "How you doing?"

"Fine," Elmer said. He walked up closer to Ben, holding out his hand. As they shook, the ex-outlaw immediately knew what the situation was. "You're on the run, ain't you?"

"Yeah," Ben said. "And I'm dawg-bit to boot."

"Dawg-bit?"

Ben held out his arm. "It's festering, Elmer. I need a doctor."

"There's one next door," Elmer said. "But, Ben, there's word out on a fugitive. If he sees you in your condition, he'll know something ain't right."

"I look perty bad, don't I?"

Elmer nodded his head. "And smell worse." He led Ben back to the rear of the store. "But don't you worry none. There's gotta be a way to get things fixed up for you."

"I don't want to cause you no trouble, Elmer," Ben said. "But I gotta tell you straight off. I'm tuckered bad."

"Yeah," Elmer agreed. "But don't fret none, Ben. I could never forget how you took a chance and left me safe there in Fort Smith."

Ben grinned through the pain. "I see ol' Judge Parker didn't hang you, pard. How many years did he give you?"

Elmer grinned back. "Hell, none! I told the doctor and the sheriff I got shot up over a card game in the

203

hills. They didn't know nothing about that train robbery back in Little Rock. Those damn railroad detectives didn't even know we'd escaped."

Ben looked around the store. "It don't appear you went back on the owlhoot trail."

"I sure as hell didn't," Elmer said. "That last episode scared the shit outta me. I went straight as a man could. I even got a job and worked as a drummer for a while. I peddled hardware. That's how I met my future father-in-law. I called on his business reg'lar. Me and his daughter hit it off and got hitched. Later, when he took sick, I got the store here. He died a couple of years ago."

"You're married, huh?"

"Yeah," Elmer said. "I got four kids, Ben."

"Aw, hell, Elmer," Ben said. "I'm leaving. This ain't gonna be nothing but trouble for you."

"Just hold on," Elmer said. "There's a shed in the alley for storage."

"Yeah," Ben said. "My horse is hitched in the rear of it."

"That's a good place," Elmer said. "And you can stay there. In the meantime I'll see a doctor about getting some things. He won't ask no questions if I tell him I'm thinking o' selling medical stuff to folks that live out in the country. That way I can treat your arm myself."

"It's bad," Ben said.

"I'll tell him what the symptoms are," Elmer said. "The sonofabitch is a damned drunk anyhow. As soon as my clerk gets here I'll take care o' things."

"Obliged, Elmer. I truly need the help."

"Let's get you out to that shed," Elmer said. He went

to the door and looked up and down the alley to make sure there was no traffic. "C'mon, Ben!'

Ben was led to a small frame building that measured ten by ten feet. Once he was inside, Elmer closed and locked the door, leaving him alone.

The fugitive had only a couple of hours to wait. Elmer came back and slipped through the door. He had a cloth poke with him. "I got bandages, swabs, and some carbolic acid," Elmer said.

"What the hell's car-baw-lick acid?" Ben asked.

"The doc says it kills infection," Elmer said. "Now let's get to work here and cut away that old wrapping you got around your arm."

"Use this," Ben said, pulling his knife out and handing it over.

Elmer began slicing away the covering. "You still good at throwing this thing, Ben?"

"That's part o' my problem," Ben said.

Elmer removed the old shirt-sleeve. "Lord above, Ben! Look at that arm!"

The injured limb was black and swollen, the flesh looking pulpy and dead. Ben almost turned away. "It don't smell good either."

"The doc said it would be a good idea to cut a bad wound open to drain the pus," Elmer said.

"Cut away," Ben said.

"It's gonna hurt, pard," Elmer said.

"Hell, I didn't think it'd tickle," Ben remarked. "Have at it."

Elmer took the sharp blade and gently laid it against the forearm, and applied growing pressure until the weapon's edge slipped into the flesh. Pus and blood exploded outward, but some of the swelling immediately subsided.

"I didn't feel nothing," Ben said.

"I figgered you didn't," Elmer said. "Or you woulda jumped." He began bathing the limb in the carbolic acid. After giving it a generous soaking, he carefully wrapped clean, fresh bandages around it. "I don't know, Ben. There's something terrible wrong here. That smell worries me."

"It's gonna kill me, I know," Ben said. "I tried to fool myself, but I can't no more."

Elmer finished. "I'd rather die by flying lead than—" he pointed at the arm, "—than that."

"If they catch me I'll end my days at the end of a rope," Ben said.

Elmer's expression showed his sincere concern. "Oh, Ben, I wish to hell there was something more I could do."

"You done enough, pard."

"What's your plans? Where are you gonna go?" Elmer asked.

Ben took a deep breath. "I'm going back to Pleasanton."

"Your old hometown? I remember you talking about it."

"That's where all my trouble started," Ben said grimly. "And I got some scores that need settling before I check out o' this game. I'm gonna find Oren Beardsley and put a bullet in that sonofabitch's head."

Elmer was silent for several minutes. "You do what you must, Ben. I'll get you some stuff from the store to take with you. You got a can opener?"

Ben shook his head.

"I'll get you one and some canned goods. They'll last and give you some nutrition." Elmer stood up. "I'll be back by dark."

"I hope nobody takes my horse."

"Nobody'll bother him back here," Elmer said. "See you later, Ben."

Ben waited twelve hours in the shed before he could leave. Elmer came back more than once. He brought some food and a bottle of bourbon. He could remember his old pal's tastes in liquor.

Elmer returned the final time a little past ten o'clock that night. "Your saddlebags is packed, Ben."

Ben struggled to his feet. He allowed his friend to help him to the horse. "I'm truly obliged," he said, swinging up into the saddle with Elmer's aid.

"I owe you, ol' pardner," Elmer said. "You took a hell of a chance when you left me on that doctor's porch." He paused thoughtfully. "Damn! How long ago was that?"

"A lifetime," Ben said. He grinned sardonically. "At least a outlaw's lifetime, huh?"

"Yeah," Elmer said. "Ben, I never had a better friend than you. And that's the goddamned pure truth."

Ben looked down at him. "There's only two things I don't regret about my life, Elmer," he said. "One is having you for a pard."

"What was the other?" Elmer asked.

"Being able to love a certain woman," Ben said.

"Did you have a wife, Ben?"

Ben shook his head. "Nope. Nothing like that. But I did have the sweet knowledge that not only did I love her, but she loved me back."

"I'm glad you was able to experience it," Elmer said. He knew he'd never see Ben again.

Ben pulled on the reins and headed the horse up the alley toward the street. "So long, Elmer."

"So long, Ben."

Chapter Fifteen

Ben rode into Pleasanton late in the afternoon as the sun, its heat still beating down on the dusty main street in relentless waves, had begun a hesitant descent toward the western horizon.

Once again Ben's arm throbbed, and the fever in his head added to his discomfort in the hot, still air. Elmer Woods's treatment had failed to stop the infection and it had grown worse during the two days the journey from Medicine Lodge had taken. A bitter smell, its intensity sure to increase, wafted up from the now-dirty bandage around his arm. Ben knew that his own body odor, after days of not washing, was also sour and disagreeable. But such things were now of no importance to him.

The town had changed much in the past twenty years. It had spread out with a larger population, and showed every indication of having become the business center the city fathers had talked about many years previously. Larkins' Livery and Feed Store was gone, but there was another farther out on the edge of the business district. A large, two-storied frame house rested on the lot where his mother's shack had been. Other similar domiciles indicated that this had become the better section of the town as it expanded and evolved to its present size.

Ben reined in at what had been the Beardsley store. An apothecary now occupied the premises. Ben turned the horse toward the hitching rack and dismounted. After a careful look up and down the street, he walked into the establishment. A dapper, short man wearing pince-nez glasses looked at him with a hint of distaste across his face. "Yes, sir? What can I do for you?"

"I'm looking for the folks that used to own this store," Ben said.

"I am the only person who has been the proprietor of this business," he man said. He noted Ben's bloodshot, glazed eyes. "Are you all right, sir?"

"Yeah. I'm fine, thanks," Ben said. "Well, what about the Beardsleys? They had a store here once."

"Yes, indeed," the druggist said. "A dry-goods store, as a matter of fact. I bought the property from the Beardsley family about nine years ago. The father had died and the son—"

"Oren?"

"Yes. Oren," the man answered. He took another, closer look at the fugitive and sniffed. Then he spotted the bandage. "Mister, you need medical attention bad."

"Yeah. Where is—"

"That's one hell of an infection you got there."

"I reckon," Ben said. "Could you—"

"Gangrene," the druggist announced. "In the initial stages. You'll lose that arm, if it's not already too late.

You need a doctor quick."

"Is any of the Beardsleys around?"

"Certainly. Mr. Oren still lives here in Pleasanton," the man said.

"In the same house they always lived in?" Ben asked.

"As far as I know," the druggist said. "You want me to take you down to the doctor, mister?" Gangrene kills, y'know. And it's not a particularly pleasant death to rot away slow like that. And look at you. You're so sick you're swaying like a drunken sailor."

"I'll take care of it. Thanks," Ben said. He walked back toward the front door.

"Do you know Oren Beardsley well?" the druggist asked.

"I sure do," Ben said. "But I ain't seen him in years."

"Then, I should tell you that Oren Beardsley is—"

"I know where he is," Ben said. "I been there before." He got his horse and swung into the saddle, riding down the main street to turn off on an elm-shrouded lane that brought long-forgotten memories exploding into stark clarity in his mind.

Ben recalled the pathetic desire to have someone—anyone—like him; the old schoolhouse in the winter with the welcome warmth of the stove such a contrast to his mother's shack; people looking or talking down to him; good old Art Larkin who'd given him a job at the livery; pretty Maybelle Beardsley so painfully unattainable and lovely; and the cruelty of her brother Oren. All these remembrances flooded his feverish brain.

Within moments he saw the picket fence around the Beardsley home. And he could remember standing

211

outside of it wanting so desperately to be invited around to the other side. He also recalled the rocks thrown at him by Oren.

Ben slid from the saddle and had to hang onto the horn for a moment as wildly pulsating waves of dizziness swept over him. He waited for the sickness to subside before he stepped on the other side of the horse and looked up at the house.

Although freshly painted with wooden shutters added, it was still the same as he remembered it. His eyes swept from the side to the large front porch.

Ben froze still.

He spotted the figure sitting on the porch in the stiff high-backed chair. The slope of the shoulders and the tilt of the head were maddeningly familiar. Loosening the pistol in his holster, Ben stepped across the walk and went through the gate.

The man in the chair spoke. "Howdy."

Ben stared at him for a full five seconds. Fat and bald, yet there was no doubt. Here was Oren Beardsley. "Howdy, Oren."

"Who are you?"

"Don't recognize me, huh?"

Oren smiled. "I don't hardly recognize nobody, mister."

It was then that Ben noticed Oren's eyes. They were colorless and clouded over, with one drifting off to one side while the other sat still as if staring straight ahead.

Oren Beardsley was blind.

"What happened to your eyes, Oren?" Ben asked heartlessly.

"Cuba in '98," Oren said. "Caught a Spanish Mauser

bullet in the neck. They say it done something to my nerves." He paused. "Who are you, mister?"

"Ben Cullen."

"Who?"

"Ben Cullen. I used to live here."

Oren was thoughtful for a minute. "Didn't you and me go to school together?"

"When I went — yeah."

"Hey!" Oren straightened in the chair. "I remember you, sure! Didn't you like my sister Maybelle a lot?"

"Yeah. I thought she was perty."

"She still is, they tell me," Oren said. "She's married to a lawyer over in Wichita. Doing real good, he is. So damned good, as a matter o' fact, you'd think a blind brother could go live with 'em, wouldn't you?"

"I reckon," Ben said, fighting a sudden wave of dizziness.

"But they won't," Oren said. "I'm a real pain in the ass to most folks."

Ben's head cleared a little. "Sounds rough on you."

"I get a government pension . . ." He paused. "Say! Didn't you bust into my pa's store?"

"Yeah."

"And went to jail, didn't you?"

"Ten years," Ben said in a flat, low tone.

"Goddamn! You spent ten years in jail, huh?"

"Sure did," Ben said. He eased the pistol from its holster and pointed it at Oren's head.

"Ben, you don't smell too good, you know that?" Oren said. "Ever' since I lost my sight I been able to hear and smell real good. And, boy, I'm sorry to say you stink to high heaven."

213

"I reckon I do," Ben said. His thumb rested on the hammer.

"It ain't just a dirty smell neither," Oren went on. "There's death in it, Ben. What's the matter?"

"Nothing I can't handle," Ben said with forced bravado.

"I feel something," Oren said. "Are you pointing at me, Ben?"

Ben made ready to cock the pistol, but he stopped. He thought of Jim Baldwin and Arlena—especially Arlena. His mind quickly turned over how she would have wanted him to handle this meeting with an old enemy who had caused him so much pain. Ben fought these emotions while he held the revolver for several more moments. Finally, he sighed aloud and slowly lowered the pistol and reholstered it. He took a deep breath. "Oren Beardsley, if you done me wrong—well, it's all right. I—I forgive you, Oren."

The blind man didn't seem to understand, so he ignored the remark. "You want something to drink, Ben?" Oren said. "There's a lady that comes over to look after me in the evenings. She makes my meals and all. Maybe you'd like to eat with me. I got some good liquor."

"No thanks, Oren. I got to go."

"You can have a bath if you want, Ben. I got cigars if you smoke. They're good-uns. And that liquor ain't nothing to turn your nose up at. How about getting drunk with me, Ben? I get drunk ever' night."

"I ain't in the mood," Ben said. "But thanks."

Oren smiled weakly. "I don't get many visitors."

"I don't suppose you do."

"I'd be obliged for your comp'ny." There was a deep pleading in Oren's voice.

"I can't stay." Ben walked down to the gate and stopped. He turned around and looked up at the fat, blind man on the porch. "Oren!"

"Yeah, Ben?"

Ben remembered a saying that Jim Baldwin used a lot. "Live in peace."

Ben got back up in the saddle. He let the horse amble slowly up the street while he took a quick assessment of his present situation. Things were so bad that he couldn't see how they could get worse. Ben was sure to lose his arm—or worse, the poison in it would spread through his body to bring about a lingering death that would torment him like a Comanche torture. Getting proper medical care for it would not only be time consuming now, it would lead to his capture and a certain appointment with the hangman.

Either way, Ben Cullen knew that he had reached the end of his journey across God's green earth.

Maybe if he hadn't been so infatuated with Maybelle Beardsley; maybe if he hadn't broken into that store; maybe if the judge hadn't given him ten years in the penitentiary; maybe if someone had stepped forward to help him; maybe—maybe—maybe. It didn't matter anymore, his choices were now limited to just one thing:

What way would he like to die.

No doubt the forces of the law would be closing in within a few days. This would give him a brief respite that would be marked by long periods of intense pain as his dying arm continued to rot and stink in its own private death throes.

Ben couldn't face that.

He turned the horse to the nearest hitching rail and dismounted. Standing beside the animal, he waited for his chance. It didn't take long. A man riding a sleek pinto came abreast of him. Ben stepped out into the street with his pistol drawn. "Hold it, mister."

The man, his eyes opened wide in surprise and fear, abruptly reined up. "What the hell's going on here?"

"Get off that horse!"

"Are you crazy or something?" his victim demanded to know.

"Damned right. Get off that goddamned horse or I'll shoot you off it," Ben said coldly.

The man dismounted, holding his hands high. "Don't you shoot now, mister. You got the horse."

Ben slipped his foot in the stirrup and forked the saddle. "My name is Ben Cullen and I'm wanted by the law. The sheriff here will have posters on me. You got that name? Ben Cullen?"

"Yes, sir!"

"Say it, goddamn you!"

"Ben Cullen."

"You go tell the sheriff that Ben Cullen is out at the bend in Sand Creek. Is that grove o' trees still there?"

"Sure," the man answered. "It belongs to a feller named Johnson."

"That's where I'll be," Ben said. "And tell that sheriff he'd best get a posse, 'cause there's only one way I'll go into that jail o' his—feet first."

"Sure. I'll tell him, Mister—Cullen."

"Yeah. Ben Cullen. Say it again."

"Ben Cullen."

"Once more — loud!"

"Ben Cullen. Ben Cullen! *Ben Cullen!*"

"Get on now, and hurry up," Ben said.

"Sure, Mr. Cullen. I'm going over there right now."

Ben watched the man scurry down the street, then he pulled on the pinto's reins and galloped toward the end of town.

Epilogue

The posse brought Ben Cullen's body in draped across the same horse he had stolen a short time previously.

Word of the bad man's killing had preceded the lawmen into town and they rode up rather proudly among the citizens gathered around the courthouse.

The sheriff himself untied the ropes that held the cadaver in place. Then he grabbed the dead man by the hair and unceremoniously dumped him at the foot of the stone steps.

Several women, their delicate senses offended by the sight, backed away as children grinned and poked each other in their gleeful dread at viewing the body.

"Did he put up a fight?" some wag in the crowd asked.

"He shot a hell of a lot of bullets," the sheriff said. "But he couldn't hit anything."

A deputy laughed. "Yeah. It was almost like the dumb sonofabitch was shooting straight up in the air."

"But he was a bad'un," the sheriff added. "Ben Cullen was a real tough hombre."

Ben Cullen did not appear to be particularly tough.

He was evil smelling and very filthy, his dead eyes wide-open and staring at nothing. Short and scrawny, he appeared even more emaciated in death. This appearance was sharply contrasted by the husky members of the posse who stood around now giving their individual accounts of the outlaw's demise. Their larger sizes seemed emphasized by the diminutive game they had just bagged.

"Photographer coming," someone called out. "Let him through."

The man, lugging his camera while his assistant carried a two-by-eighteen board, pushed his way through the crowd and immediately set up his instrument. Meanwhile, willing hands took the same ropes that had held Ben Cullen to the horse and used them to strap his corpse to the piece of lumber.

After the slat bearing the dead man was propped up, the posse posed one by one with the bullet-riddled corpse. Following the individual photos, they had their pictures taken in pairs. Finally each had his likeness made with the sheriff to record the incident for posterity.

Another hour of activity passed before the undertaker arrived with his wagon. A couple of strong men picked up the pitifully light dead man and dumped him onto the bed of the vehicle. They left him lying in an awkward position, face-down and pigeon-toed.

It didn't take long for the crowd to disperse after the undertaker left, and Ben Cullen was the topic of most conversation even though the town was getting back to its usual business.

As a port is to a sailor; a nest to an eagle; or a den to a wolf; is death to an old outlaw: Home.

The run was over.